Today was not the day they died.

Jerking the back door open, he hauled Sailor out. "Run."

Dragging her by the hand, he threw his body over a low wall, bringing Sailor with him to land on top, cushioning her fall. He rolled over to protect her with his body as a fireball of heat and debris shot over them, shaking the city block.

Pieces of the department-issued sedan rained down.

He let his forehead drop to touch Sailor's. "That was close."

Gabe pulled Sailor closer to his chest. It could've been her. He could have lost her.

He'd been without her for eight years and would've bet his favorite signed baseball that he could get two inches from her and still walk away. Coming face-to-face with losing her permanently twice in such a short amount of time had shocked him into reality.

"Gabe, what about the CDs?"

He pulled out the huge envelope. "Someone wanted these gone badly enough to try to blow us up. Now we just need to figure out who."

Books by Stephanie Newton

Love Inspired Suspense

Perfect Target
Moving Target

STEPHANIE NEWTON

penned her first suspense story—complete with illustrations—at the age of twelve, but didn't write seriously until her youngest child was in first grade. She lives in Northwest Florida, where she gains inspiration from the sugar-white sand, aqua-blue-green water of the Gulf of Mexico and the many unusual and interesting things you see when you live on the beach. You can find her most often enjoying the water with her family, or at their church, where her husband is the pastor. Visit Stephanie at her Web site, www.stephanienewton.net, or send an e-mail to newtonwriter@gmail.com.

MOVING TARGET

STEPHANIE NEWTON

Steeple Hill®

Published by Steeple Hill Books™

STEEPLE HILL BOOKS

Steeple Hill®

PLEASE RECYCLE
THIS PRODUCT IS RECYCLABLE

Recycling programs for this product may not exist in your area.

ISBN-13: 978-0-373-44351-2

MOVING TARGET

www.SteepleHill.com

Printed in U.S.A.

I have come that they may have life,
and have it to the full.

—*John* 10:10

For Mom, who took me to the library every week
and shared her love of romance…and for Dad,
who encouraged me to read and shared
his love of suspense.

Thanks to Melissa Endlich, my wonderful editor,
for choosing this book and working with me.

To Barbara Collins Rosenberg: thanks for giving
this book of second chances one more.

Many, many thanks to my critique partners
and readers: Catherine Mann, Elizabeth White,
Holly La Pat, Brenda Minton…you are priceless.

To Allen and the kids: you make my life beautiful.
Thanks for putting up with this crazy writer's life.
I love you.

ß

ONE

A shot blasted through the quiet night.

Her dog erupted in barking. Sailor Conyers whirled around to face the French doors leading to the balcony of her art studio. Nothing but inky blackness outside.

She took several deep breaths and grabbed for Scruff's collar. That sounded close. Too close.

Her heartbeat thumped against her chest. Maybe it wasn't really a gunshot. It could even have been a car backfiring. Definitely, a car. Or maybe someone had fired at one of the snakes that sometimes strayed too close to a front porch. That made more sense than her overactive imagination. This neighborhood wasn't the same as the one she grew up in.

With shaking hands, she forced herself to pick up the shells and place them gently in the grout that edged the mirror. Midnight was so not the time to be artsy-craftsy. Exhaustion from working all day in the coffee shop kept her from being as precise as she wanted to be.

The sound she heard was probably nothing.

Scruffy paced in front of the wide balcony doors. The hackles on the back of his neck crept up to stand on end.

One long tooth showed out of the side of his mouth as he growled low in his throat. He obviously hadn't gotten the memo that it was just her imagination. "You're not helping, bud."

She shoved a piece of coral into the grout. Therapy. This was therapy. Eight years ago, her pastor had suggested that finding a hobby would help her relax and find the peace she needed to deal with the past. It worked. Most of the time.

But not tonight. She'd grown up in a poverty-ravaged area far from the tourist-driven economy on Sea Breeze Beach. She knew firsthand that the sound she'd heard wasn't an ancient car in need of servicing. But she could still rationalize it.

A second muffled shot popped. Her hand jerked, knocking seashells to the floor, shattering them at her feet. That was no snake shot.

Sailor called the dog, an increasing urgency to move away from the windows making her palms sweat. She shoved the jagged pieces out of her way with the side of her foot and hurtled for the stairs, skidding to a stop halfway down.

The dimly lit first floor of her cottage looked slightly sinister from up here. Scruff growled behind her.

"Way to inspire confidence, mutt." But she scratched behind his ears, glad that she happened to be keeping him this week for her brother and new sister-in-law while they were on their honeymoon.

At the bottom, she grabbed for the cordless phone. Through the front window, she could see the back side of the coffee shop here. Her carriage house had once been the garage for the old Victorian her partner had turned into a coffee house. A light had been left on upstairs. Her office? She'd locked that up hours ago. A shadow passed in front of the shade in her office, and the light went out. Goose bumps prickled her skin. What had she seen?

Four halting steps took her to the front door, where she checked the dead bolt, pushing the numbers nine-one-one on the handset as she slid the bolt home.

"What's your emergency?"

"I heard shots fired…and I think someone might have broken in my business."

"Is your address 1312 Beach Drive?"

"Yes, I'm in the carriage house behind the main building. Across the street from the beach."

"Are you okay? Would you like me to stay on the line?"

"I'm fine, just…hurry, please."

Sailor hung up the phone, keeping it clenched in her hand. She was afraid to look out the window. Her surroundings, usually so reassuring and cozily familiar, failed to comfort. With her heart in her throat, she took the sure path into her bedroom.

The lockbox stayed beside her bed disguised in a wooden chest. Her hands were steady now as she lifted the box. She didn't hesitate as she turned the dial to the correct combination to release the catch. She picked up her Beretta and checked the load and the safety.

Sailor knew what she was doing. She had trained every Friday for years. Fear, pain and loss were part of her past, not her present. It wasn't part of her agenda, not for today.

She was *really* sure she hadn't penciled in "terrorized by gunshots" in the midnight slot.

She couldn't quite bring herself to sit on the couch in the open, chose instead to sit at the bottom of the staircase by the front door, the gun on her lap. Scruff laid his big head on her knees.

She laced her fingers into his thick black fur and held him tight. "Hang in there, big boy. Help's on the way."

Gabe Sloan craved the rush of adrenaline. High-speed kite-surfing, parachuting out of a plane so high he needed oxygen, sneaking into enemy territory. He'd done all of that and then some. But the call over the radio that sent him to the home of his high school sweetheart…that was a call he never wanted to receive.

Of course he knew with both of them in tiny Sea Breeze, Florida, he was bound to run into her—he just hadn't expected to care. He flipped on the bar of red and blue lights. As beach patrol, he drove a truck, hauling a surfboard in the back for rescues. It was a long way from a Humvee at Baghdad International. Or an armored SUV in Kalabi, Africa. Gabe smiled and gunned the powerful engine.

Sailor Conyers. His best friend since she'd come crashing into his hiding place under the big oak tree with two cowering kittens she'd rescued from the neighborhood bullies. He and Sailor had pretty much been inseparable through middle school. High school, too. She'd been his first crush, his first clumsy kiss.

And she was the reason he left home.

He turned onto Beach Drive, nearly deserted this time of night, and narrowed his eyes at the darkness. The tall streetlights were out down the long street.

Weird in the well-cared for tourist area, even this time of year. The hair on the back of his neck prickled.

Not even questioning his professional sixth sense, he eased on the brakes, flipped the car lights off, and pulled to the side of the road a couple of doors down. He'd learned the hard way never, *never* to ignore the hair prickle. The first time he'd felt it, he'd been on an op. A gunshot wound, nineteen stitches, a round of anti-biotics and a whopping tetanus shot later, Gabe decided he might listen to that hinky feeling next time.

He slid out of his car and into the dark. A wet breeze blew curls of white fog around the oak trees surround-ing the boardwalk businesses. Low clouds covered what moon there might have been, leaving dark shadows among the eerie ghostlike tendrils creeping across the road from the Gulf of Mexico.

Gabe unsnapped his holster. Tires easing onto gravel at the edge of the street signaled his partner's arrival. Shots fired could be completely accidental or it could mean big trouble. No officer would walk into such a situation alone, not even Gabe. After four years in the Army and three working as a private military contractor, he understood the power of teamwork—if the situation called for it.

Joe Sheehan fell into step beside Gabe, the ever-present mirrored sunglasses hanging on a strap around his neck. He spoke softly, his voice not carrying beyond Gabe's ears. "Any idea what's going on?"

"Nope." As Gabe walked, he kept to the grass at the side of the driveway, so his boots wouldn't crunch on the oyster shells. He wasn't mentioning his itchy feeling. Joe might understand it, but then again he might rag him about it for the next twenty years or so.

"It's quiet."

"Yeah, things are calm now." So why did the back of his neck still tingle?

Sheehan touched his shoulder. "I'll hang back, take a look around. You go to the door, check on Sailor."

"You know her?"

"Of course. She's the lieutenant's sister. And I have coffee here all the time. She's got the best blueberry scones in town." Sheehan's soft chuckle belied his alert stance. Seconds later, he had disappeared around the side of the tiny carriage house and Gabe Sloan stood at the door to his past.

He knocked. "SBPD."

The door flew open. "Thank goodness you're here…*Gabe?*"

She moved toward him, almost as if she wanted to hug him, but she faltered back, and pink crept onto her cheeks.

"Hi, Sailor. Good to see you. Sorry it had to be these circumstances."

Good to see you? Was that even true? It seemed like the right thing to say. He hadn't seen her in nearly eight years. Since she'd cut him out of her life as completely as if he'd been surgically removed.

He'd lost her as a girlfriend, and that had hurt. But it was losing his best friend that had nearly killed him. He'd wanted to make up and tried to figure it out with everything his seventeen-year-old self had, but once she left home, he couldn't even find her to try.

When he'd left for basic training a month later, there hadn't been anything to keep him in the area, certainly not his family. And when he'd moved back—well, she hadn't been first on his list to see.

"Sailor?" She was still staring at him. A huge black dog growled at her side. He returned her gaze, struggling for a stranger's polite non-look. "You okay?"

"Yeah, it's just…my brother Cruse told me you were back home working for the department, but seeing you is…wow."

"I know." She hadn't changed much. Her hair was a little darker blond, her features a little more defined. Still, it was a kick in the gut to see her. One he hadn't expected. "Can I see your weapon, please?"

She looked at her hand as if she just realized she was holding a gun. Then she blinked twice, and handed him the weapon. "Scruff, release."

The dog gave him an irritated look and stalked to the rug in front of an empty fireplace.

"You called about an intruder?"

Sailor motioned to a dark brown leather chair and turned to face him.

He didn't sit. The space was clean, calming, and looked nothing like the Sailor he remembered. Her room, even in the dump she'd lived in, had always been a riot of color and hand-painted furniture. One summer afternoon, she'd even made him hold the ladder while she'd stenciled bright flowers and loopy green vines along the ceiling.

This woman looked the same, same blond hair and sweet face, but her ocean-colored eyes were wary. She cleared her throat, watched him walk around her room. "I'm sorry to call the emergency number."

"You did the right thing. What happened?"

"I was working upstairs in my studio when I heard a shot. At first I thought it could've been nothing—or nothing worth reporting—but when I heard the second one, I made the call."

"Was there a break-in?"

She hesitated. "I saw a light on in the main building. Upstairs in my office."

Gabe paced to the window, looked up. "It's out now."

"I know."

"Did you fire your gun?"

"No." She worried her bottom lip with her teeth before explaining. "It's for my protection. I train at the range. You're not going to keep it, are you?"

"I don't think so." He laid it carefully on the mantel above the spotless fireplace. She wasn't getting it back until he could figure out what was going on here. "Has anything happened recently that would make you think that you would need that kind of protection?"

"No." She didn't qualify the bald statement, but he could figure it out.

A knock at the door had her jolting.

"Easy." Gabe held a hand out to steady her, jerking his hand back as he touched her and memories rocketed through him. They'd climbed trees together. He'd steadied her on her feet hundreds of times. "It's Joe Sheehan. He's been checking around back."

Joe's light gray eyes lit with a smile when he saw Sailor. He held a fist out for Scruff to smell.

"Did you find anything?"

"Nothing that couldn't be explained by the daily traffic through here." He shot a serious glance at Gabe. "You ready to check out the main building?"

Sailor reached for the doorknob. "I'll go with you."

"No." Both men spoke simultaneously.

"I own the coffee shop. I'm going."

"It's safer to stay here, Sailor." Joe's expression would put a pious priest to shame. *Hello, good cop*.

"Please." She looked at Gabe.

He shrugged. "Stay out of the way."

When Joe shot him a look, he added, "It's her property. And if she's as stubborn as she used to be, she'll follow us anyway."

Gabe walked out the door without looking back.

Joe followed. "The lieutenant will have our badges if anything happens to his sister."

"I'll take responsibility." Squinting up at the old Victorian, Gabe saw nothing, no movement, not a single light.

"It's my call. *I'll* take responsibility." Sailor stalked beside him, the dog running ahead to the door.

Gabe suppressed a smile. Yeah, she still had a strong-willed streak.

The dog pawed at the door and it squeaked open. Gabe's muscles tensed, instantly alert.

"Uh-oh." Sailor's whisper was nearly soundless.

Beside him, Joe drew his gun.

"I don't suppose you left the door unlocked?" Gabe drew his own weapon and moved to the other side of the door.

"No." The low clouds shifted, leaving moonlight suddenly streaming around her. Her green eyes met his, worry and something more—the edge of anger—in them.

For the first time, he felt a smile tug the corner of his mouth. "Don't worry. I'll protect you."

Sailor faltered as Gabe disappeared into the building, Joe right behind him. He'd said the exact same words the first time they'd met. She'd crashed his hiding place with two undernourished kittens, trying to escape the boys who'd been torturing them. Gabe had been ten years old and as lean and scrawny as those poor cats. He'd been afraid. Yet the first thing he'd done was puff up his chest and offer to protect her.

They'd been inseparable from that day until the day they broke up. She'd thought she was in love with the minister's son with the café-au-lait eyes and the bring-it-on attitude, but didn't all teenagers think their love was destined to last forever?

Ancient history now. She could handle seeing Gabe, would have to handle seeing him. He worked with her brother.

He'd changed so much. His hair still had a tendency to fall over his forehead, but its light brown had deepened to chestnut, with golden highlights glinting in the overhead light. His body was still lean, but he'd broadened in all the right places. The shoulders were wide and strong, his arms ropy with muscles, waist narrow.

In his tactical police uniform and body armor, he looked tough. Hard. She needed to remember that when her memory pegged him as the lanky kid whose parents were too busy to bother coming to his baseball games.

Obviously, given his words, Gabe's memory hadn't faded any more than hers had.

From inside the building she heard, "Clear."

It was followed by another, deeper in the house, "Clear."

Sailor stepped into her kitchen, the heart of her business, and closed the door. Still clean and cozy, smelling mildly of fresh-baked cookies and coffee beans, it didn't look like it had been disturbed. The front rooms—the sitting rooms—held small tables and chairs, couches and reading areas. Nothing looked out of place.

She was so tired. Maybe it really was all in her imagination.

At the staircase to the offices, she met Gabe coming down. The stony look on his face, far from that of the reckless warrior of a few minutes ago, scared her. She tried to push past him.

His strong hands gripped her upper arms, holding her in place. "Sailor, you don't want to go up there."

Panic crept into her throat. Her voice stretched thin. "Yes, I do."

She jerked away from him, running up the stairs, tripping and catching herself. As she lurched past her now-dark office, she saw the light on in the guest room next to it. She skidded into the doorway and into Joe's massive chest, but not before she saw it—him. *Oh, Charlie.*

The sight and the tangy smell of blood overwhelmed her, and she gagged.

"Get her out of here." Joe pushed her to Gabe, but she pulled away.

"Sailor, you can't go in there." Gabe's voice was firm, but not harsh, authoritative and in control, so different from the emotions careening inside her.

"I need to." She resisted the urge to flee, to run as far and as fast as she could. "He was—he was mine," she finished helplessly.

"He was her business partner." Joe crossed his arms, still not moving.

"It's a crime scene." Gabe pulled her toward him,

zeroing in on her eyes. "Sailor, look at me. Your being involved with the victim has other implications."

She whipped a look back at Joe. *"What?"*

He sighed, nodded.

Gabe, her oldest friend, but still so much a stranger, held her hand. "I think I'm going to have to take that handgun, now."

TWO

Sailor had been questioned repeatedly and seen the looks of disbelief and suspicion from these men and women—cops—most of whom were friends. Her story was going to stay the same, no matter how many of them asked her, or how many times she told it.

"I didn't kill him." She said it to herself as a crime scene tech hurried down the hall with her gun in an evidence bag.

"Nobody thinks you did." Gabe's deep voice rumbled behind her left shoulder.

"Then why are you taking my Beretta? And that guy over there said they would need my fingerprints." Her voice spun up, but it was easier to think about that than what was really going on behind the door to the guest room. She rarely slept there and she couldn't remember the last time her business partner had stayed the night.

"The techs will test-fire your gun to exclude it as the murder weapon. But you knew that, didn't you?" Gabe propped against the wall, arms crossed over his chest.

"I don't know, I guess." A tremor ran through her body, and she wrapped her arms around herself. "Who would have killed Charlie?"

"Why don't you tell me?"

"I don't have any idea. He was like—everyone's favorite uncle." She closed her eyes, tried to pray, but the words wouldn't come. She didn't even know what to pray for. She shivered again.

Seconds later, a blanket dropped around her shoulders.

"I'm not cold."

"Okay, suit yourself." Gabe shrugged, reached behind her to straighten her favorite Mose T watermelon painting, and walked away.

Her chattering teeth made a liar out of her. She shuddered uncontrollably, but she didn't want to think about the reason she couldn't get warm. Why couldn't she get the vision of Charlie out of her mind?

The last thing she wanted was Gabe's sympathy. He unsettled her, in this place she'd made her sanctuary. If his actions tonight were any indication—bucking his partner and letting her enter the coffee house with them—he still had that impulsive streak. And after growing up in chaos, she craved order and stability.

She wouldn't get it tonight. Sailor flicked a glance back across the hall where the crime scene unit gathered evidence in the upstairs bedroom, a leftover from the time the house had been a home.

At some point, she'd have to call her employees and tell them the business would be closed tomorrow. But not yet. First she had to get through this horrible endless night.

"Ma'am, if you'll come with me?" A man of around forty dressed in plain clothes, but with a badge hanging around his neck, stood at her elbow.

"May I ask why?"

"I'll need the clothes you're wearing. And I'll need some other samples. This shouldn't take too long, but I'll have to be thorough."

Heat started at the base of Sailor's neck. She'd do this for Charlie, and she'd known it would be hard. She just didn't think it would be so humiliating. She rose to her feet and gathered the quilt around her.

"Hold it right there." Gabe's voice shot through the crowded hall. "Where are you going?"

The crime scene processor raised himself to his full five-ten, which seemed quite small next to Gabe's six-two. "We need what she's wearing to exclude her as a suspect."

"Where's Fuentes?"

"Busy." The guy squirmed, but to his credit, he held eye contact.

"Call her over."

"No."

Gabe stared the smaller man down until finally the CSU investigator rolled his eyes and stalked to the door of the bedroom, Gabe at his heels.

Within seconds Maria Fuentes appeared in the door. The short, feisty forensics specialist who worked with Sailor's brother had gone to high school with Sailor and knew Gabe from the neighborhood. She listened to her officer and then nodded at Gabe, holding up one narrow finger. The plain-clothes investigator left without a word.

Gabe turned toward Sailor, his chest broad underneath the bulletproof vest and tactical gear.

Melted caramel eyes locked on hers from down the

length of the long, wide hall of the old house. She'd been such a fool to think that somehow if she ignored him long enough that he would disappear—as if the time with him had never existed. He'd been her best friend. How could she think that didn't matter?

The frenetic activity around them seemed to simply fade. The flash of the crime scene photographers, the murmur of the cops' voices, the people weaving in and out of their line of vision, all of it just faded away as Gabe started toward her.

One step and then another. Out of habit, her fingers twisted into her necklace, the charm nestling into her palm. Even as a young man, he'd drawn her, but the truth was, the years only made him seem bigger than life now that he was here in front of her.

Gabe gripped Sailor's shoulder with a heavy, reassuring hand. "Maria Fuentes will be out in a few minutes. You know her, right?"

True to her word, ten minutes later the forensic evidence specialist strode through the door, stripping off latex gloves. All of five foot three, corkscrew curls flying, Maria Fuentes zeroed in on Sailor like a pelican on a hapless fish. Except when she got to Sailor, her expression gentled. "Okay, sweet pea, what do you say we get this over with?"

Sailor'd been given sidelong looks all night from the cops—some friendly, but more of the glances showed suspicion and curiosity. Now met with genuine kindness, she blinked back tears. She didn't cry, ever. It just wasn't worth the effort, even for momentary relief. Whenever it was over, you were still left where you were in the beginning, with the same problem you started with.

She stood. "Where do you want to go?"

Maria scanned the room. "Hey, Rodriguez, you done with the hall bathroom?" At his affirmative grunt, she waved a short jewel-free hand at the bathroom door. "In there will do. They'll go over it again when we're finished."

Sailor held the quilt around her like she might lose some piece of herself if she loosened it. After the night she'd had, she wouldn't count it out.

Gabe watched Sailor slip past Fuentes into the bathroom, grasping the blanket a little tighter around her shoulders. She was in shock. Anyone would be after finding a friend and business partner murdered in cold blood.

She'd huddled in that chair blindly staring at the door to the bedroom, shivering until he'd covered her with a blanket. But he couldn't care about her. Any feelings he'd had were for the girl, not the woman, and those had died a long time ago with a Dear John letter that had found him in Kandahar nearly a year after he left for basic. He'd known it was over. The letter had just been the final nail in the coffin.

He had other priorities in Sea Breeze now, like being a good cop, making a difference in his old neighborhood, making amends of a sort with his past. Against all odds, he'd found faith in the most unlikely of places. He had to come home to put it into action.

Maria came out of the bathroom and aimed herself at Gabe, handing evidence bags to a waiting tech as she did. She snagged the cup of coffee Gabe hadn't been drinking anyway and took a big swig. When he made a token protest, she raised an eyebrow. "You asked for me. You could've had Sparky over there. Explain to me who appointed you her protector."

"I was the first responder. It could just as easily have been Joe Sheehan."

Maria stared into his eyes, assessing him—or maybe his motives—before she shrugged. "She could be in trouble. That room isn't Charlie's normal bedroom. He only sleeps here occasionally. You know her office was trashed?"

"You've got techs in the office, too, right?"

Maria swigged coffee and handed his cup back. "Yeah, and thanks. Three a.m. comes a lot harder than it used to." She paused. "Gabe, the intruders didn't bother trying to make this look like a robbery. Charlie Banks is wearing a three-thousand-dollar watch. I think Sailor could've been the target."

The image of Sailor with blood pooled around her like Charlie Banks swam through Gabe's mind. His vision went red at the thought of someone hurting her on purpose.

"She's going to need protection."

"Put her in a safe house. At least until her brother gets back in the country," Gabe suggested.

Maria smiled her feral-cat smile as Sailor came out of the bathroom wearing borrowed SBPD sweats. "I talked to him. He wants you protecting her, hotshot."

The Army had trained Gabe well, but one thing he excelled at was close protection. He'd spent most of the last few years in an obscure African country, making sure the president of that fledgling democracy lived to carry out his duties. If someone was targeting Sailor, he could keep her safe until that person had been identified and neutralized, but there were at least a dozen other options. Apparently, none of which suited his lieutenant.

He blew out an exasperated breath. "Fine."

"Fine. In the meantime, brace yourself. It'll be tough on her until the GSR test is in."

"The field test was negative. It seems ridiculous to make her the brunt of suspicion and gossip." Gabe felt like punching his hand through the wall. Used to action, standing around and not being able to change the course of events had his skin itching. "Unless she's a criminal mastermind, there's no way she could've pulled off killing him and getting back to make the call, not without leaving some evidence."

"I know that—and so do they." Maria gestured to the cops still milling around the upstairs of Sailor's house. "We all know Sailor and love her. Which is why we're going to take care of her in the only way we know how—by clearing her."

"There are other suspects. He had a son and a girlfriend that I know of."

Maria shot him a sideways glance under her lashes. "We'll take a look at them, too, though good luck getting to the girlfriend. Layla Grady's been the golden girl of the mayor and chamber of commerce ever since she opened that souvenir factory here." She hesitated. "I didn't have the chance to tell you before, but I'm glad you finally decided to come home. It hasn't been the same around here without you. Have you seen the old neighborhood lately?"

Gabe froze, then eased back against the wall. Maria

couldn't know anything. Even the permits were under the corporate name. "Ah, yes. The anonymous developer. Does it look good?"

"I never knew lower-income housing could look so nice. I would've given my right arm to grow up in a neighborhood like that instead of the—well, anyway. What brought those wandering feet home?"

Gabe shook his head. "It was just time."

Maria followed his gaze to Sailor. The CSU cop's soft chuckle drew his attention back to her. "Yeah, I guess it was. Why don't you offer her an escort home?"

Gabe started to tell Maria it wasn't like that, but it wasn't worth the bother.

And she'd soon discover for herself that Sailor was nothing more than an old friend who happened to have crossed his path.

He found Sailor braced against the wall, shadows deepening around her dark green eyes, strength of will surely the only thing holding her upright.

"If you're ready to go home, I think we can kick you loose until tomorrow."

She jolted as she heard Gabe's voice and it took her some time to find his eyes with hers. "I'm not sure I want to go there by myself."

"I was planning to walk you home."

She stayed quiet until they reached the door, walked through her tiny house, and found everything relatively undisturbed. The police had been through it, but unusually—probably out of respect for her brother, the lieutenant—had left things pretty much the way they'd found them.

She walked Gabe to the front door of her cottage,

Scruff at her side. Silky blond hair seemed determined to slide forward over her shoulder.

She shoved it back again, managing a wisp of a smile. "Thanks for bringing me home, and for sticking up for me tonight with the CSU guy when you didn't have to. I guess it's just another in a long string of times that you've come to my rescue."

She glanced behind her at her house and pulled the door closed behind her as if she could re-close the door on her life to keep it from his view. "Gabe, what was between us was over a long time ago."

Over.

Right. He'd wanted to put the past behind him. To put a period on that part of his life, so to speak. To go on to what God had for him now. A whole *new* life.

So, yeah, he knew it was over as much—more—than she did. But he reached for her hand, playing with her fingers for a few long seconds. Without giving her warning, he pulled her to him, wrapped his arms around her and snugged her to him. She still fit, just there, under his chin. His heart pounded an unsteady rhythm as she leaned into him.

She sighed—a soft, sweet sound. "*Gabe,* what are you doing?"

He had no idea. "Comforting you?"

Obviously she heard the chuckle in his voice, because a half-exasperated laugh slipped out. "I'll be okay, thanks. I've been on my own a long time now."

He pulled back from her. Risk assessment was part of his former job, second nature now. This one was a no-brainer. A man *happened* to be murdered in a room that Sailor *happened* to frequent. Her office had been tossed. He deemed it highly likely that Sailor was in danger.

"I'll see you tomorrow, Sailor. There will be more questions. I'm sorry, I know it's a lot to think about." And in the meantime, Gabe would be plastered to her 24/7, whether he liked it or not.

"Can I get a skinny mocha latte?" The beefy cop lowered his voice and looked around.

Sailor reached for a cup. "Sure, you want whipped cream?"

His voice dropped to a whisper. "Can you put it in a cup with a lid?"

Sailor nodded soberly. "Absolutely."

As the happy detective walked away, hitching up his belt, Layla Grady leaned on the granite countertop next to Sailor. "You're giving it away, aren't you?"

Sailor shook the used grounds from the scoop into the compost trash bag. "I slept for a couple of hours and when I came back over here, the cops were already here, so I started making coffee. I know it's weird, but I think Charlie would've enjoyed this—the crime scene tape, a shop full of cops. He'd have been right in the center of it, handing out coffee and muffins."

Charlie's longtime girlfriend cleaned the steamer nozzle with a thin white rag. Her lips curved into a sad smile. "I don't know where else I would be."

"You don't have to stay. I know it's hard."

Layla placed a beautifully manicured hand over Sailor's plain-Jane fingers. "Charlie wouldn't have liked you being alone to handle all this. And I feel close to him here."

Shifting away, Sailor opened the wide door of the commercial oven on the back wall, checking on the mini muffins. "It's going to be so different."

She told herself that the moisture in her eyes was from the heat of the ovens, but she knew better. She'd been trying to keep busy to keep her mind off the fact that she'd only slept two hours. Off the fact that she'd lost her father figure and mentor in one cruel blow. Off the fact that she had no idea what would happen now.

She owned forty-nine percent of a business. As long as Charlie held the remaining fifty-one percent, she'd been fine with that. But with his share most likely going to the son, things were going to change. Ken hadn't had any interest in the business, but even if he wanted to sell it, she couldn't afford to buy him out.

Since her crazy childhood, she'd lived her life to avoid unanswered questions. But here was a chance to trust God with her future. He always came through, so why did she feel so alone?

Maybe because those pesky unanswered questions about the future wouldn't leave her in peace.

"Could I get something extremely large and caffeinated?"

Sailor's head jerked up as the deep voice hit her memory full on.

"Need room for cream?" Layla's southern drawl deepened to honey.

Assured Gabe was in good hands, Sailor slipped out from behind the counter to check on the rest of the place. Even with few customers, flat places tended to collect empty cups and the magazines got tossed around.

Because Sip This had once been an old house, she and Charlie had kept the original character of a home and left the front sitting area a cozy gathering area. The deep-cushioned sofa and chairs invited. The folk art pieces she'd picked for the walls charmed, and as always, the earthy smell of coffee pervaded the senses. An unexpected wave of grief hit Sailor so hard that she sank down on one of the couches and let her head drop. *Dear God, what am I going to do without Charlie?*

He had taken so much joy with every piece she bought. As the shop took on her personality and identity as well as his, he had surprised her with the offer of limited partnership—an offer she hadn't had to think twice about. She had loved working at the coffee shop, so being an owner had been a no-brainer. But what would happen now?

A warm hand settled between her shoulders. Familiar somehow, and comforting, even when she knew she should be rejecting it. She knew she'd walked away from Gabe eight years ago for his sake. With everything that had happened, leaving him had nearly destroyed her. And afterwards, she'd worked so hard to stand on her own. To rebuild her life.

He'd hurt her—badly—and she hadn't given him a chance to make it up, or explain. Maybe she owed Gabe—an explanation, if nothing else. But could she afford to risk the peace that it had taken her years to painstakingly piece together?

The faith she'd found then had sustained her through some incredibly trying times. She had to believe it would carry her through any circumstance.

She sighed and lifted her head. "Gabe—"

The heavy oak front door crashed open, shaking the glass in the windows and the art on the walls. Always one for the entrance, Kenneth Williams Banks stormed into the coffee shop, the coat of his stockbroker suit flapping behind him. Chaos with a capital C, Ken didn't get along with Sailor on a good day. And he was the last person she wanted to deal with today.

Gabe reached for his service weapon, the move instinctive, as Sailor jerked to her feet. He didn't take his hand off her back. Instead, he stepped up behind her as a thin, suit-clad man strode in like he owned the place.

The man's dark brown eyes zoned in on Sailor. "Sailor, what's going on? I thought at least my father's death would warrant closing?"

Ah, the son. So maybe he did own the place.

Gabe could feel Sailor's muscles bunch under his hand, but she didn't bolt.

"I am closed, Ken. But taking care of the people here—I think that's what your dad would have wanted."

"You think he'd have wanted for his loved ones to not even be able to grieve because of strangers tromping through their space?"

Sailor leaned back almost imperceptibly into Gabe's hand. The trust implied in that gesture loosened something in him. Eight years, lots of rough water under the bridge, how did she know she could?

The truth was she didn't. But she trusted him anyway.

She cleared her throat. "If you want me to close the shop for a few days, I'll make the arrangements, but I can't throw out the cops who are here now, even if I wanted to. I can stop serving them, if you wish."

Her sweet tone made Gabe want to laugh. He'd heard that same tone often enough growing up to know that Ken Banks would get his way now, but somehow, someway, he'd regret it later.

He glanced at Sailor. Elegant in unrelieved black, with her blond hair swept into a smooth knot at the base of her neck, she had fatigue circles under her green eyes from lack of sleep, but she was beautiful, strong.

Why was he surprised? He'd grown up over the last eight years. Why would it be any different for Sailor? Maybe because in his mind she'd stayed the same innocent girl he'd known, an innocent who'd broken his heart with little apology, when he'd only been trying to do the right thing for both of them.

Gabe gritted his teeth, prepared to wade into the conversation and bodily remove Charlie Banks's son, if necessary. This guy—even if he had the excuse of being grief-stricken—was at the least a big jerk. Gabe would also call him a "person of interest" in the case. Someone he would be talking with before long.

Banks straightened his lapels and blew out a breath, his shoulders relaxing a tiny fraction under the suit. "You know what, you're right. He'd have wanted coffee brewing and cake baking and forget what I preferred."

The younger man scrubbed a hand over suddenly weary features and swayed toward Sailor.

Already wary, Gabe shifted his weight forward.

Ken grabbed for Sailor's upper arm. "Excuse me. We're having a private discussion here."

Gabe moved Sailor out of the guy's reach. "Not anymore, you're not."

"Gabe." Sailor's voice warned him that he was

stepping on her toes. She pulled away to slide her arm through Banks's. "Why don't you let me fix you a macchiato? I know you must be parched after your drive, and we'll talk about how you want to handle things the next few days."

Gabe watched Sailor lead the grieving son, still with a rod in his back, into the back room. He'd almost dismissed them when he caught the shrewd look the stockbroker cast up the stairs when he thought Sailor wasn't looking.

Tentative, anxious, grief-stricken. Those looks he could understand. After all, the man's father had been killed upstairs. But cunning—not such a normal reaction to the sudden loss of a loved one.

And in Gabe's mind, that made Ken Banks suspect number one.

THREE

Sailor looked out the wide front window at the gray late-afternoon sky. The girl was still there on the porch. Dressed in an overcoat, shaggy jeans and several layers of clothes that looked like they hadn't seen a washing machine in a long time, she huddled in one of the over-sized chairs. She didn't fit the profile for Sailor's usual clientele, but she pulled the strings of Sailor's heart. If not for Charlie's generosity, she might have been that girl.

Since Gabe had finally disappeared, Sailor poured two cups of coffee and slid out the front door. The teen seemed to shrink in the chair as Sailor approached and eased into the chair next to her.

"Hey." Sailor placed the coffee on the table between the two chairs and nodded at it. "Help yourself."

"I don't need charity." The young woman pulled an off-white knit beanie farther down over a tangled mess of curly chestnut hair.

"I didn't say you did. But it has to be something like thirty degrees out here with the windchill and it happens that we're giving coffee away today. If you don't want it, though…" She moved to pick up the mug.

"Wait." The girl reached for the cup with surprisingly clean hands. "Thanks."

"So, why aren't you home with your parents and out of this nasty weather?"

"Don't have any parents." Her chin came up, even as she stuffed her free hand into the pocket of her overcoat.

Sailor fought a nearly overwhelming desire to take the girl inside and feed her. Parents didn't always act the way they were supposed to, and when they didn't, they left a wake of sorrow behind them. She had reason to know. "My name is Sailor. What's yours?"

"Chloe."

"Are you in trouble? I've got a house full of cops here that can help you if you need it."

Chloe's eyes darted back to the door. "No, don't bother. I was just trying to get out of the wind."

Sailor held her mug in both hands, letting the warmth of the coffee seep into her chilled fingers. She looked at Chloe, recognized the red-rimmed eyes, runny nose. She'd lived with her mother too long not to know the signs. But the girl's skin was too pink and pretty for her to be too much of an addict.

Maybe her nose was running from the cold November wind. And maybe Sailor would win the fifty-million-dollar Florida lottery tomorrow—even though she hadn't entered.

"Look, I think you're probably a good kid, but this isn't a halfway house." The girl's shoulders dropped, but still she had something a little heart-strong in her expression. Something that reminded Sailor of another girl, who sat in that exact spot, eighteen and pregnant, in front of Charlie, daring him to hire her. Daring herself not to cry if he didn't.

She fought a smile. "If you want to hang out here, you'll have to work. I'll give you odd jobs and pay you for them."

Chloe's face held a desperate mixture of hope that Sailor meant what she said and the certainty that the deal was too sweet to be true.

"There's a condition."

"I knew it." Chloe exploded to her feet, and stomped two feet away, her arms closed in on herself. "I knew you weren't going to hire me."

"You have to stay clean. That's it. That's the only condition. And I *will* check."

Chloe went still. She looked at her feet for a long moment before meeting Sailor's eyes for the first time. "Okay."

"We're going to be closed for a day or two because—" she still stumbled as she said it "—because of a death in the family, but I could use a dishwasher. You interested?"

A quick nod.

"Here's the name of a church that opens at night when the temp drops below forty degrees." Sailor scribbled it on a scrap of paper she pulled from her apron pocket, and held it out. "Ask for Jake."

Chloe's hand brushed Sailor's as she took the note. "Thanks."

"You bet. I'll see you in the morning." She stared after Chloe's retreating back.

The window behind her screeched up. "So, you think that was wise?"

"You spying on me, Gabe Sloan?"

"Trying to keep you out of trouble."

"It's really no concern of yours whether it was wise or not. Until I know otherwise, this is still my business to run, and taking that girl in is what Charlie would have wanted."

"You're gonna get your heart broken."

"Maybe." She shivered, suddenly wishing for her coat. "Okay, probably. But sometimes people just need a chance."

The window slammed down.

Gabe stopped at Sailor's side a few seconds later and draped her coat over her shoulders. "You're right, Say, sometimes people do need a second chance."

Sailor dropped into the chair that the street rat had just vacated. Gabe turned to look at the beach. The fresh air in his face, cold as it was, braced him. The rush and crash of the stirred-up ocean mirrored the tangled feelings that just being near this woman brought out in him.

As Gabe propped against the porch rail—blocking as much of her from the street as possible—she peered up at him. "Why are you here?"

"I'm doing my job."

"Yes, but why this job?"

He started to give her the easy answer. The one that rolled out with no thought at all. He'd been an Army Ranger. He'd patrolled the perimeter at Baghdad International. He was good at being a cop.

All that was the truth, but it wasn't the reason.

"I joined the Army because I thought it was my only option." He slanted a look at her, and guilt lodged in her stomach—a hard, heavy knot of regret. "It turns out that I kind of had an affinity for the work. I was good at being a soldier."

He hesitated, spoke more quietly as Sailor continued to stare across the street at the tumbling sea. "All that time in my father's home—it took a young African man named Kitengi sharing an extreme faith for me to understand what a real relationship with Christ meant. When I was in Africa working security, he led me to Christ."

A beat of silence. "And what brought you home, Gabe?"

"My grandparents died." He heard her sigh of sympathy, but he couldn't look at her. He didn't like talking about his grandparents or the inheritance that had seemed like a noose around his neck until he'd figured out he didn't have to actually keep the money. "I didn't make things right with them before they died. I never lived up to what they wanted for me."

"They were hard on you, Gabe. They paid for that fancy private school for you, but they couldn't pay for your love and respect."

She remembered as well as he did. His chest hurt, thinking about those old wounds, old hurts that still had the power to sting. "I've made mistakes, too, Sailor. It's too late to resolve things with my family. But it's not too late to resolve things with you. We were friends."

She crossed her arms. "Yes, we were, but we were kids."

"Why did you break things off, Sailor? Why did you leave that night?"

She stooped to pick up an olive shell someone had

dropped on the porch, brushing the sand off the smooth, shiny surface. Was she avoiding answering, or persuading herself to tell him what he needed to know?

When she looked at him, her ocean-green eyes were stormy like the Gulf on a really bad day. "I was raped, Gabe. I needed your support more than I'd ever needed it in all the years we were friends."

He wasn't some sensitive dude, not by a long shot. But something about the way she owned her pain made him hesitate to push her further. That day would be seared forever in his mind. While he'd gone to the park for a pickup game of baseball, she'd gone home. She hadn't known her mother's boyfriend would be waiting for her.

Gabe hadn't known their lives—both their lives— would be changed forever. He softened his voice. "I thought I was sticking by you. We went to tell my dad we were getting *married*. The next thing I knew you were gone."

He'd promised her forever. Yes, he knew that she'd been raped. He'd wanted to marry her, not because of it, or in spite of it, but just because he loved her, even joining the Army so he would have a way to support the two of them. But something changed on the night they'd gone to break the news to his parents.

He stabbed a hand through hair already standing up from the heavy, salt-laden air. If he was honest with himself, part of him had been relieved when he saw her again last night. That he *could* get closure because he could finally be there for her in a way that he hadn't been in the past. In his gut, he knew he'd failed her somehow—he just didn't know how.

He'd been too young, too inexperienced to know

what to do then. But he knew—*knew*—they'd had a connection. And now he wasn't some green kid. He could get to the truth. He could be the protector that he couldn't be then.

And then he could move on.

Sailor faced the beach. "I was standing outside in the hall like we planned, while you told your dad."

She stopped, chewed on her lip, stared hard at the turbulent waters of the Gulf of Mexico.

"What happened, Sailor?" Gabe prodded gently.

"I heard you talking. You told your dad how we were planning to get married and how you had enlisted." Her voice had gone husky with the remembered hurt, and suddenly Gabe realized he didn't want to hear this, but he had to. He'd wondered for so long what could've been big enough to take her away from him, from the future they'd planned.

"I told my dad I loved you." He wanted to reach for her again, to care for her in the one way he could, by just being here, standing by her like he'd wanted to so many years ago. But he couldn't do that for her, because she didn't want him to.

When she spoke again, her voice was so quiet he had to lean close to hear her words over the sound of the breaking surf across the street. "Yes, you did. And he said that you were confusing love for sympathy and compassion. That you minister to people like me, you don't marry them."

The truth was like a bullet searing his heart. "He was wrong, Sailor."

"I was so ashamed. You had plans—a scholarship and

the chance to play ball in college—before I was attacked. Your father was right. You did feel sorry for me."

Guilt and shame warred within him, hurt and anger mingling with it to form a toxic brew of feelings. "What happened to you, the place you grew up, the attack, none of it was your fault."

"Don't you think I know that?" Frustration laced her voice and she prowled to the edge of the porch, hanging on to the column like a lifeline.

"I don't know. Do you?" He stepped up beside her, careful not to touch her.

"Yes. But Gabe, it would have been my fault if I'd forced you into marriage and made us both miserable. Cruse took me in so I wouldn't have to live at home anymore."

The last thing he wanted was to make things worse for her. She'd left that night and he'd moved heaven and earth to find her, only leaving when he had to report to the Army or be considered AWOL. Some of it made sense now, she'd been hurt and scared, and her brother the cop had kept him out of the loop.

"It wasn't like that for me. I was in love with you, Sailor."

"I loved you, too, Gabe. That's why I couldn't marry you."

Gabe looked down to find his fingers clenched around the porch railing. Yeah, he was hurt that she hadn't trusted him with the truth. Angry, too, at himself that he hadn't been there when she needed a friend. And she still wasn't telling him everything; he could see it in her eyes.

Reaching in his pocket, he pulled out the promise

ring. She'd had one just like it. A claddagh ring, the symbol of love, loyalty and friendship. At one time, he'd thought they'd had it all.

Maybe they hadn't really. Maybe his parents and her mother and all they'd grown up with had damaged them more than he'd ever imagined. For sure, *his* love hadn't been strong enough for her to trust him.

Scratched and dull, it had been a talisman he'd carried with his pocket change all these years. Why? Maybe he'd kept it because he still held her as some ideal of the woman he was looking for. Maybe because she'd been his first love.

When he looked up at Sailor, her eyes were fixed on that small piece of tin in his hand, her hand at her neck. "It's just a thing."

"You kept it," she whispered.

For years, he'd figured he'd kept it as a reminder of what not to do again. Not trusting a woman with your heart, not trusting a woman to stick around. He'd wondered for so long. He shoved the ring back in his pocket. He had part of the answer now.

"Come on, I'll walk you home." He glanced both ways, scanned the scrub across the street along the beach. They were clear.

She fell into step beside him, trusting him to protect her.

He had faith to carry him through. In his darkest moments, when death seemed to stalk him, it had been enough. It would be enough now. He knew that his God was strong enough to carry any burden—if he let Him. All Gabe had to do was let go. God was strong enough to take care of Sailor, too.

But for now Gabe was her protector. And she

needed to know he would stick by her. Not because he had to, or because her brother was his boss, but because he wanted to.

The door to her carriage house stood wide open. Sailor pushed forward, faltering to a stop on the threshold. She stood, swaying, as she took in her wrecked home. Every drawer had been pulled and tumbled, every cushion shredded, every book torn off the shelves. The house still stood, but it looked like a force of nature had ripped through it.

Gabe's wide shoulder brushed hers as he stepped up beside her.

"Why?" she whispered. She'd worked so hard to build a life, to create a place where she felt safe, where she didn't look over her shoulder every second.

"It isn't random." His voice was hard, not like the Gabe she knew, his warm brown eyes flinty cold. "What do you know? What do you have, or what do they *think* you have, that could possibly cause this?"

"I don't know! Don't you think I've been trying to find some clue to why Charlie was killed? I don't know what they're searching for. If I did, I would just give it to them."

"It took some guts to strike here with a shop full of cops right next door. Or maybe it was just smart. Why would it be protected with so many uniforms nearby?"

Fear struck like a fist in the gut. "Gabe, what about Scruffy?"

She'd left him at home thinking he'd be in the way at the shop. Why hadn't she brought him along?

He grabbed her hand, dragging her into the house. "Stay behind me."

Staying out of his shooting range, Sailor followed Gabe through the tiny house, shivers coursing through her. Scruffy wasn't in his usual spot by the fireplace, wasn't closed up in the coat closet, wasn't under her bed. "He's not here."

"Maybe he's scared. Call his name."

Though she scoffed at her brother's big dog being afraid of anything, she whistled for him as Gabe ran up the stairs. "Come on, Scruff. Come here, boy."

From above, she heard Gabe's strained voice. "Up here, Sailor."

Her heart tumbled as she saw Gabe kneeling on the floor of her studio by the huge dog, pushing through the thick pelt of hair. She dropped to her knees beside them.

"Scruffy. Hey, boy. Come on, you big lunk." Her voice croaked around the lump in her throat. "Does he have a pulse?"

"Shh." Gabe felt around some more, pressing with his fingers. Scruffy didn't move. No wagging tail, or cold inquisitive nose. His beloved tennis ball, well-chewed, lay on the floor beside him.

Tears welled in Sailor's eyes. She'd lost so much. She couldn't lose Scruffy, too. The dog belonged to Bayley and Cruse, but spent many days with her in the coffee shop while they were at work. "Please, Scruff, be okay."

She closed her eyes, a silent prayer all she could think. *Please, God, let him be okay. Please, God.*

Gabe pulled back the dog's lip, showing his big eye teeth, then sat back on his heels. "He's alive. His oxygen level looks pretty good, but his pulse is a little slow. I'd guess whoever came in your house tossed him some raw meat with a sedative in it."

Sailor sniffed back the tears, wiping a swift hand across her eyes. "He's just a stupid dog."

"Uh-huh." Gabe gripped her hand. "If he doesn't look any better in a few minutes, we'll take him to the vet."

Sailor looked at her clenched fingers. She was so determined to make it on her own. But she needed someone, something just now. She'd take sympathy and compassion even if that's all he could—or would—give.

She ran her thumb over a scar that crisscrossed the top of his hand. He twitched, but didn't pull away. "What happened there?"

"Ah—a little altercation with a rebel leader. It's no big deal."

"No big deal would be stubbing your toe. Or getting a big strawberry bruise from sliding into home." Something she'd seen him do a thousand times.

"I kept all my fingers. That was the important thing."

"Oh, Gabe." She couldn't imagine being in a situation where a good outcome was keeping all your appendages, but she could imagine the sense of helplessness that came with having your life in the balance, purely at someone else's whim. And while she'd been here building a life, he'd been in the thick of danger.

"I was in trouble. The rebels were trying to negotiate for some weapons that my team had seized. It could have meant tying the rebel leaders to illegal arms and—possibly—finding their supplier."

"What happened?"

"I got rescued." Not before the rebels tortured him for four days. "My team got me out of that mess, Sailor."

He tucked a stray piece of hair behind her ear. "Me and Joe, Maria, and everyone else on the SBPD, we're going to get you out of this one."

Her breath hitched out a long, emotion-driven sigh. She'd never been able to depend on anyone but herself, but somehow, when Gabe said it now, she wanted to believe it.

He stood, turning away to prowl the small studio space. She'd taken so much pride in organizing her house, a far cry from the constant turmoil of her childhood. Everything she owned had been placed just where she wanted it. And everything had been pawed through, ripped open, broken. The wooden shelves in here had been full of apothecary jars holding shells and beads, small found items—things she used to create her art. They were in jagged pieces on the floor.

She'd needed her faith to get through what had happened to her, to the other side of the pain, to rebuild a life that hadn't been much to start with. To have to start over…it was hard not to feel abandoned by the very God that had brought her this far.

She pulled Scruffy's head onto her lap. He mattered, not the debris around her. She ran her fingers through his soft fur, as Gabe made the call to Maria to get the CSU team out there.

As he hung up the phone, Gabe kicked through the scattered remnants of her ordered life. "Why don't you paint anymore?"

Her hand stilled on the dog's fur. How could she explain that picking up a brush brought back memories, horrible memories that she couldn't suppress? "I just don't."

Cruse had tried to help, even finishing this upstairs space for her and buying her all those canvases and paints, but she couldn't bring herself to brush on the first stroke.

Gabe's caramel eyes were too knowing.

She looked away as Scruffy's tongue snaked out to lick her hand. "Gabe."

The big German shepherd lifted his head from her lap and laid it back down with a thump.

Gabe sprayed water into a bowl at the wash-up sink in the back of the room. Kneeling down beside them, Gabe spoke softly as he lifted Scruffy's head. "I bet you have a headache, huh, bud?"

Even with Scruffy awake, Sailor felt an underlying tension coiling like a spring inside her. Someone was targeting her, stalking her, invading her life and her space. They'd killed her friend. What were they planning for her?

Tires on the oyster-shell driveway sent her eyes searching for Gabe's.

"Relax, it's probably Maria. She'll be in here yelling at us for messing up her crime scene within minutes." Gabe didn't smile. The corner of his mouth tilted, but there was no sign of his generous grin. "When she takes over the scene, we can leave, take Scruff to the vet or whatever you want. But you can't stay here tonight. You might want to put a few things in a bag."

Her spine shot straight. "No."

Gabe got to his feet and leaned over her. "Listen, whatever it is you don't know or don't remember, something set all this in motion. What happened to the guy that raped you? What happened in Charlie's past, or his son's past, do you know?"

A quick negative jerk of the head.

"Until we find out, you can stay with Maria."

"I don't want to impose on Maria."

Gabe crossed his arms. He wasn't in uniform today, but it didn't seem to matter. He looked massive and immovable. "Okay then, you're sticking with me."

Before she could argue, heavy feet pounded up the stairs. Gabe pulled Sailor to her feet and shoved her behind him. The dog wagged his tail.

"I think she'll be sticking with me." Her brother stepped through the door, his green eyes laser-sharp and just as deadly.

Sailor pushed past Gabe to hug Cruse. "I would say that you shouldn't have come home early, but I'm so glad you're here."

Cruse wrapped one arm around Sailor, anchoring her at his side. "Thanks, Gabe. I'll take it from here. We can talk tomorrow."

Gabe hesitated, clearly reluctant. He'd been a solid presence, guarding her, even helping her deal.

A new kind of panic rose in her. This had been her safe place. Her sanctuary in a crazy world. She'd created it that way and now every protective shield was crumbling.

She didn't need Gabe, didn't want him. But in just two days, she was already growing to depend on his strength again. She was in big trouble.

And not just from the bad guys.

FOUR

The water softly lapped at the hulls of the big charter boats lining the wharf at the marina. The sky pinked in the east and Gabe sucked down convenience store coffee. He'd spent the previous two hours trying to sleep and failing. Restlessness brought him here to the marina where Charlie Banks had lived.

The boat bobbed in its berth. No old clunker, Banks had kept his fifty-foot fishing yacht spit-shined. Yellow crime scene tape kept the boat off-limits for now. Until they figured out exactly what happened to Sailor's boss, no one knew what might be a clue. Gabe removed the tape and stepped on board.

Instantly his senses flooded with memories of his grandfather and deep-sea charter trips meant to turn Gabe into a "man's man." Gabe hadn't been strong enough, mean enough or man enough to make his grandfather happy. Now as an adult, Gabe realized that he hadn't been the son that his grandfather had always wanted, the son his own father hadn't been. The expectation had been created before he was even born.

And Gabe could let it go, learning from his African

friends to respect his elder family members even if he didn't agree with them—or want to. He had inherited more than money from them. He could thank his grandfather for his work ethic and his father for his compassion for other people, even if it hadn't extended to him. Both were worthy attributes he could be grateful for.

The boat rocked, a not-so-gentle jolt that wasn't created by the early-morning charter traffic. Someone had broken into the cabin.

Adrenaline surged through his system, making every sense keener, more alert. The dust from the crime scene processers on the doorknob had been disturbed. On television, cops were always busting doors down. In this case, opening the door quietly would be much more effective. Pulling his weapon, and locking it in a two-handed grip, he swung the door open.

Layla Grady had the desk drawers open, papers strewn all over the place, her arm in the middle drawer up to her elbow.

"Sea Breeze PD."

Layla's shoulders jerked. She looked up and smoothed her features into a docile, yet somehow purely female look of contrition. "You caught me, Officer Sloan."

"Why are you here, Layla? This boat has been sealed pending investigation."

"I'm so sorry. I know I shouldn't be here. But I couldn't find a photograph Charlie kept of us from a trip to the Bahamas last year. It's a favorite."

Layla in jeans and a sweater was somehow more vulnerable than the dressed-to-kill Layla he normally saw. Even more so with tears welling in her eyes.

"I needed a happy memory to hold on to, especially today." One glistening tear trailed down her cheek.

Gabe put his gun away. "Understandable, but you're going to have to leave now."

She tucked a strand of highlighted hair behind one ear. Couture and cultured, she reminded him of his grandmother, who had been more interested in what her garden club thought of her than her own grandson. But regardless of his personal feelings, Layla was grieving a personal loss.

She reached to the bed for her coat. "I'll get out of your way, but if you find the photo, would you mind bringing it to me?"

"Sure."

Layla slid past him in the galley area, only to stop as she reached the door, fiddling with the ties on her pink trench. "It seems like there are more and more senseless acts of violence these days. I'm almost scared to live alone."

"You should be fine. Someone wanted to kill Charlie. It wasn't a random accident."

She blinked wide blue eyes. "I just can't imagine it. Did you know that I never once filled my car up with gas when I was with Charlie? Even if he was taking a charter group out, he would get up at four in the morning to go to the gas station if he knew my tank was low."

"He sounds like a person I would have wanted to know."

"Thanks, Gabe. Bye now." The door swung open and he watched her effortless jump from the stern of the boat to the pier. It would be so easy to underestimate

Layla. She had a perfectly reasonable explanation for being on the boat, but he certainly wouldn't cross her off as a suspect. Her guileless eyes and fashionable looks disguised a sharp, savvy business sense and a very fit fiftysomething figure.

Out of the corner of his eye, he caught movement rounding the corner of the office building across from the marina. It happened fast, but he could have sworn he saw the off-white beanie and all-black Salvation Army look that Sailor's protégée Chloe favored. It didn't make sense for her to be here, far from Sip This, and even farther from Christian Community, the church that ran the shelter.

Too many questions existed about Chloe. He didn't know her last name. It seemed like too much of a coincidence that she had shown up at Sailor's shop the day after Charlie Banks's murder. And while he had created the townhomes on the site of their old neighborhood for people exactly like Chloe to start a new life…something just didn't add up about her. But one thing he could say for certain. If there was something to discover, he would dig it out.

Used to waking in the dark hours of the morning, Sailor tread softly heading from her bedroom in Cruse's beach house to the coffeepot. This morning, it wasn't work that had her unable to sleep. Charlie was the closest thing to a father she'd ever had. And today she had to say goodbye to him. As she stepped into the living area, she stopped short when she saw Bayley already in the kitchen.

Her sister-in-law smiled, tightening the sash of her

short terry-cloth robe. "I figured you'd be up early. I've got the kettle on."

As Bayley poured the steaming water over tea bags, Sailor settled on a stool at the kitchen island. It had only been a few months ago that Bayley had been on the run from a stalker and Sailor had comforted her with tea in this very spot.

"I'm sorry about Charlie." Bayley's never-fail directness rocked Sailor's already shaky control.

"It's a shock, losing him like that." Sailor's voice trembled, and she steadied it before going on. "I don't know what's going to happen now."

Bayley rounded the island and had an arm around Sailor before she'd even finished her sentence. "I don't know, either. But what I do know is that God has a plan, even in the most difficult of times. Just like I know it's hard to keep trusting when things seem so difficult."

Sailor's eyes filled and she blinked the tears back. Tears solved nothing. Hadn't she learned that so many years ago? They didn't feed her when she was hungry, they didn't stop her mother from drinking, or her brother from being angry and hurt. They didn't stop her from losing one of the only things in her life that mattered…her friendship with Gabe.

"I'm scared, Bayley."

"You should be." Her brother strode into the room, his expression fierce. "I just got a call from Maria Fuentes. They've finished processing both the room where the murder took place and your office. Everyone has been excluded."

Sailor gulped her tea. "What does that mean?"

"Either the killer left no evidence—which never

happens—or it was someone who had reason to have been in that room before. Someone Charlie knew."

Her mug clanged on the granite countertop. "That means I probably know the killer, too."

Cruse gave a short, grim nod. "I'm not going to let anything happen to you, Sailor. I promise."

"I know you're going to try."

Bayley pulled her closer as Cruse gripped her chin, tilting it up. "I *will* protect you."

She loved her brother. He'd spent much of his adult life feeling responsible because he hadn't stopped the attack on her before it happened. Never mind that he had moved away from home and couldn't possibly have known. He felt accountable. And maybe he saw this as an opportunity to make up for the past—her past.

Sailor placed a gentle hand on his chest. "Cruse, you can't always protect me. You *can* always be here for me—just like you always have been. And that's more than enough."

"Did anything happen in the week before the murder? Anything that made you suspect something was going on with Charlie?"

"I already answered these questions for the police the first night."

"Humor me."

Despite the overwhelming urge to run far and fast away from the two of them, Sailor searched her brain. "I really have no idea. The only thing that would possibly be different is that I ordered an audit. I was trying to figure out what the most profitable areas of the business were so we could capitalize on those. Make sure we weren't being wasteful. You know."

"No strangers hanging around, no threatening phone calls, hang-ups?"

"None."

"We're going to get to the bottom of this, Sailor."

"I know. Charlie deserves that much, at least." She went silent. "Do you ever wonder about your father?"

"No." Cruse's expression went instantly flat.

"I do sometimes. What my father would do if he knew he had a daughter."

"Honey, you know that he was only a means to an end for her—a fast way to get cash for her next fix. You were named Sailor because all our mother could remember about him was that he was in the Navy."

"I'm named after my dad." A half laugh came out more like a sob. "I would have gladly taken Charlie's name. If he did something that got him killed, it won't matter to me. He treated me like a daughter and I loved him."

Bayley wrapped her arms around Sailor. "He loved you, too. You know he did."

She nodded. Bayley had gotten the happy-ever-after that she deserved. It didn't happen that way for everyone. Sailor was living proof of that.

And she knew as well as anyone that things didn't always work out for the best.

Gabe detested funerals, hated the pomp and ceremony that some people believed went along with death. Hated the smell of funeral arrangements, hated the false grief that some people thought hid their curiosity. Most of all he hated that he had been to so many.

Charlie Banks's funeral wasn't really an exception to

the rule. He went to a more casual beach-style church, but people were the same everywhere. And there was a weird mix of people here, all of whom Gabe would be keeping an eye on. If Charlie Banks knew his killer, chances were someone here knew more than they were telling.

Layla stood to the left near the first row, perfect in a trim black suit, perfectly poised, far from the grieving widow he'd seen this morning. Beside her, stony-faced, sat stockbroker boy, Ken Banks.

To the right were a group of guys all in black suits. They could be the pallbearers, but because they were all dressed too much alike, Gabe would guess they were from Ken's office. The question was, among these people, who had something to gain from Charlie Banks's death? It didn't seem likely that it was one of those stick-straight men.

Sailor didn't sit in the front row with the family, even though she'd admitted she'd been like a daughter to Charlie Banks. In fact, she sat alone, almost as if she had an invisible wall around her. If he hadn't known her, he would've guessed all that beauty hid a cold heart. The smooth twist to her hair, the aloof expression. He might've guessed that the unrelieved black was in deference to the occasion, but he hadn't seen her in any color, not once in three days.

She'd been so vibrant, so alive as a kid. And as a teen, she could light up a room just by entering it. He knew what happened to her. He knew that it hurt her then and haunted her still, but that spark was still there. Glimpses of it still emerged in that stubborn streak of hers, like the determination to hire a homeless teen.

He observed the crowd as the music started. Watching as Cruse and his new bride slid into the pew next to Sailor. The L.T. would never have told Sailor this, but he'd made immediate arrangements to fly home when Gabe called. He would guard Sailor with his life. But still Gabe felt compelled to see this through—to be able to stand by Sailor through the investigation, to use his skills to keep her safe now when he hadn't been able to as a kid.

Ken Banks rambled through a eulogy, his hands jittery as he gestured. He had an alibi for the night his father had been murdered. But alibis weren't ironclad. According to Ken, he had been at a bar with friends. A simple matter to slip away, especially if they had been drinking. Which one of Ken Banks's friends would break and give Gabe a clue?

As the pastor of the church delivered a message, Gabe studied Layla again. She'd been out of town on business. He'd checked. She was registered at the hotel where she said she'd been, but no one could remember seeing her. Her business associates had, but her meetings had been the next day.

Sailor's shoulders were strung tight as a bow as she stood and walked to the podium. Her knuckles were white as she gripped the edge, the morning sun streaming in huge windows warm on her back. "I didn't have a dad."

She stared at her notes and cleared her throat. In the back row, Gabe stood, not even sure why.

Sailor cleared her throat again and started over with her eyes firmly locked on Gabe's. "I didn't have a father growing up. I didn't know what it meant to have someone on my side. Someone who delighted in my successes simply because they were mine."

She spoke almost as if he were the only person in the room. "I never had a father to teach me things, to show me how to be a better person. To show me how to steam the perfect froth for a latte." This drew a chuckle from the crowd and Sailor's shoulders relaxed. "But Charlie did. He brought me to church. He taught me to fish. He did teach me to steam the perfect froth for a latte—and how to run a business. But most of all, he taught me to laugh again. He was the only father I've ever known."

Gabe saw her glance to the first row and catch sight of Ken. She stumbled over her words, searched for Gabe's face again. "He was also my friend when I needed one, like he was for so many of you. And like you, I'll miss him forever."

She walked to the edge of the platform, her high-heeled sandals clacking on the wood planks, and stepped off onto the carpet, sliding back into the seat beside her brother. But it was Gabe she turned to look for.

Futility built inside Gabe, explosive and noxious. He wanted to institute a lockdown in the building until a killer confessed. End this here and now for Sailor. But all he could do was stand beside her.

The pastor, Jake Rollins, closed the service and the friends of Charlie Banks milled around, talking.

Sailor had managed to hang on to her composure through the service, but as the various well-wishers, many of them customers and friends, stopped to talk to her, she started to tremble. Gabe plunged into the milling throng in the aisle, pressing through until he could stand beside her.

Layla Grady broke away from the group gathered around her and came to Sailor, both hands outstretched. In her suit, Layla appeared to be the quintessential southern lady. "Sailor. How're you holding up, sweetie?"

"I'll be fine. I've got the coffee house to worry about—until I know what Ken wants to do with it, anyway. He doesn't seem to want much to do with me, so I don't know if he'll want to remain partners."

Layla patted Sailor's hand. "Honey, I know you miss Charlie—we all do. But he wouldn't want you grieving him. He'd want you to be happy. He always said so."

"I can't just let it go." Sailor gripped Layla's hand. "He deserves justice, and I promise, I won't stop until I find out what's going on. I will find out who did this."

Gabe spoke quietly at her side. "You don't have to do it alone, Sailor."

Layla folded Sailor into a hug, but Sailor didn't move. "And don't worry, honey. I'll get Ken to come around."

Gabe touched Sailor's elbow as Layla turned away. "Come on, let's get out of here."

Sailor let Gabe lead her back through a few lingering groups of people to the door.

"What did Layla mean, 'I'll get Ken to come around'?"

She didn't want to talk about it, instead tilted her face to the warm sunlight.

"Sailor?"

She sighed, waved a dismissive hand. "Charlie wanted to be cremated. I'm not invited when they go to scatter the ashes. Ken's always had this crazy idea that

I stole his dad from him. The truth is that he alienated Charlie every time Charlie tried to reach out to him."

"Does Ken benefit from Charlie's death?"

He wasn't looking at her. He was scanning the parking lot, his eyes narrow and sharp. "I don't know. What are you thinking, Gabe?"

"Murders are committed by a family member or someone close to the victim something like ninety-nine percent of the time."

He tucked Sailor into the car, slamming the door behind her. As he got in on the other side, he said, "What's Layla really like?"

"She's smart and steel-strong. She started making these shell-covered picture frames and candles in her basement. Now Sand Dollar Souvenirs employs fifty people and ships all over the country."

"Impressive. Would you call her a friend?" Gabe checked the rearview mirror and whipped around a corner. He didn't think anyone was following them, but he didn't want to risk it.

"Yes and no. We don't have that much in common. It's the people and relationships that I love about the coffee shop. For Layla, business is all about the challenge."

He pulled up in front of a half-constructed beach place and she could see him relax just a fraction. "My house. I'm living in a condo in Pensacola while it's in progress, but I spend a lot of time here, weekends and stuff."

She wandered under his house. Like most if not all of the beach places on Sea Breeze Beach, the house was built on wooden stilts with a concrete slab underneath.

There was an outdoor shower still being built, and a storage area, along with a picnic table. She could guess what he did on the weekends—a canoe and a couple of kayaks hung from the beams.

"So you're planning to stay?" Did she want him to? She couldn't be sure, but she held her breath as she waited for his answer.

"This is home, Sailor. I had roots here and I'm putting down more. I've missed the water, couldn't quite get it out of my system." He held out a hand. For a moment she stared at it. Could she pretend that this was a simple walk on the beach with a handsome guy?

He'd untucked his white shirt and it hung loose over his khaki pants. His feet were bare, toes in the silky, white sand. She could see the shape of his weapon under the soft linen shirt.

She grasped his hand with tentative fingers, kicked off her shoes. "I forget to walk on the beach."

"I know. It's easy when you're busy." He skimmed a finger down her cheek. "I'm sorry you've had a rough day."

The wind pushed his shirt up, catching the soft fabric on the hard edges of his gun. He loosened it to let it fall back in place.

"Why are you wearing your weapon?"

"The simple answer is that you're in danger." He turned toward the edge of the sand, where the surf skittered and ran.

"And the not-so-simple answer?"

Gabe went silent, for so long that she thought he wasn't going to reply. "My dad was a big bear of a man, a real tough guy. He had to be, taking people in off the streets. They were all addicts, or wounded somehow. My dad handled them all, not with his fists, but that booming voice. Eventually he would share his faith with them. I don't think my dad was afraid of their threats. But as a kid I was."

The gulls screeched and dove in the stiff November wind. Sailor squeezed his hand. She'd always been able to count on Gabe for the truth even if it hurt. And though she'd known his dad, she hadn't known the reality of living with him.

"I told you I joined the Army to support us when we got married. But when I signed on the dotted line, I knew I would learn the skills so that I would never be afraid again."

She'd been topsy-turvy in love with him and when he asked her to marry him, he made her feel like the attack on her didn't matter to him. *She* mattered. Of course, she found out later that he was just trying to do the right thing for a friend, and whatever else she doubted now, she didn't doubt that he'd been a friend.

"So did you learn how not to be afraid?"

"No. But I learned that it actually kind of called to me, creating safe havens for people around the world." He shrugged again, kicked at the sand.

"You're still doing it." Surprise stole across his face—that she would realize it? "Not like your dad did, though."

"No. My father put his ministry first, no matter what. I won't sacrifice the people I care about for a calling. I'm still idealistic enough to think I can do both."

"But you were willing to sacrifice yourself for me."

He stopped, the sand squeaking underneath his feet as he pivoted toward her. "What are you talking about?"

"You were willing to marry me, even though you didn't love me, just because you thought I needed someone to take care of me."

The rough-and-tumble waves reflected in the dark surface of his eyes. "I asked you to marry me *because* I loved you."

For a while, she had thought that she'd put all of the pain of the past behind her, but here she was again. She shook her head, all the emotion of the last few days meshing inside her on the same crazy roller coaster. The grief, the uncertainty, and most of all the unanswered questions.

Was she being unfair? "We were kids, Gabe. Your dad was right." She took three steps back from him.

He reached for her hand, only succeeding in grabbing her fingertips. "My father made that comment, not me."

"I didn't hear you disagreeing."

His face a thundercloud, he turned away from her, toward the water, muscles bunching in tension. "What do you want me to do, Sailor?"

What did she want? An admission, or apology? For what? They had been kids caught in a situation that neither of them had been responsible or prepared for. But if she were honest with herself, she'd wanted him to stay, to fight for her. And he hadn't. He hadn't even answered her letters.

Her heart beat staccato-style in her chest. "Nothing, Gabe. It's all in the past, anyway."

She pulled her fingers out of his grip. Helpless exasperation all over his face, he stretched out upturned hands. "We were friends, at least. Is this all there is left?"

"I don't know, Gabe. I wish we could be friends again, but I don't know if it's possible." She backed away from him, pulling her cell phone out of her pocket. "I can't do this, don't *want* to do this now. I'll call Cruse to pick me up."

She turned and walked away.

FIVE

He watched her back, straight as a rod, as she walked away. If she sniffled a little, or battled tears, he didn't see them.

All this time, he'd wondered. And now he knew for sure. She'd believed what she heard his father say. And she hadn't heard what his own heart knew—that the deep, strong love he felt for her had been real. And at seventeen, he hadn't even known how to fight for her.

So it had started with a thoughtless comment by his father, who had spurned all of the family wealth, but still had enough prejudice in him to want his only son to marry well. His father had no idea how deeply those careless words had cost Gabe.

But in Sailor's mind, it was Gabe who had let her down, Gabe who had failed to stand up for her. Digging his hand in his pocket, he found the ring, rubbed it gently between his fingers. It had been all he had of her.

She had no idea he'd left home that night and stayed with a buddy from his baseball team because he couldn't bear to be under the same roof with his parents. His hypocritical father and his mother, who, even though she focused on her ministry, was way too self-absorbed to be a mom.

Tires skidded on the oyster-shell street behind him. He jammed the ring back in his pocket. That noise was not right, not here. Not in this beach town where cops like him wrote tickets for people going five miles over the speed limit.

Sailor, a distant figure, disappeared under his beach house. The canoe fell first, and Sailor tumbled. He heard the gunshot crack then, and he knew.

"Sailor!" Already in a full-out sprint, he reached her within seconds, but seconds might as well have been hours. She lay still on the concrete flooring, legs sprawled out at an unnatural angle. The canoe had struck her. Had the bullet?

Blood coursed down her face from a deep crease in her forehead. Gabe ripped off his shirt to expose his T-shirt. Balling it up, he pressed it against her wound.

He fumbled in his pocket for his cell phone, dialed nine-one-one. The operator was infuriatingly calm as she took their information. As Gabe hung up, he struggled for some semblance of calm, but he couldn't grasp it.

He couldn't calm his heart rate, thumping an erratic pattern. He'd let her walk away. Just like eight years ago when it had been a pickup game in the park that kept him from going home with her. He'd let her leave and she'd been vulnerable. And just like eight years ago, she'd been horribly harmed.

He looked up at the clear, blue sky, a heavy black knot in his chest. *Dear Jesus, what had he done?*

"Gabe."

His partner's voice barely registered.

"I heard the call on the scanner. Can I do anything?"

Gabe resisted the urge to move the shirt and check Sailor's wound. "Get the ambulance here faster."

Sirens sounded in the distance.

"Did you see a car before the shots were fired?"

Gabe turned back to Sheehan. "No. I didn't see a car at all. I *heard* it come around the corner. It didn't sound right, so I started back this way, but I was too late. I saw the canoe fall, Sailor fall, and then I heard the gunshot."

The other officer shook his head. "She was lucky. If he hit her instead of the support for the canoe, she'd probably be dead."

"Believe me, I'm fully aware of that." He smoothed the hair away from Sailor's face as the ambulance turned into the oyster-shell driveway, siren abruptly stifled.

The EMTs jumped out of the cab as Joe stood to wave them over. With their equipment on a gurney, they rolled double-time toward Sailor.

He gave them the abridged version and backed away as they went to work on Sailor, trying to stabilize her.

Gabe clenched his fist around his old promise ring, depending on the familiarity to soothe his ragged temper, but it didn't help. He wanted to slam it through a wall or windshield. Anything to release some of the unbearable tension that came from playing the "what-if" game.

He'd replayed the moment when he'd let her walk away from him at least a hundred times in his head. Every time he reached out to grab her hand and held her there. He could have stopped her. It was his fault this happened. He didn't protect her when he could have.

He'd let her down. Just like before.

"Did you discharge your weapon?" Joe's words cut into Gabe's thoughts.

"No." Gabe pulled it out from the fast-draw holster behind his back, the one he wore when off-duty, and held it out to Sheehan. "Whoever it was had disappeared around the block before I got to the street. And I was more interested in helping Sailor at that point, anyway."

He'd been in a blind panic.

Instead of studying the weapon, Joe Sheehan studied Gabe. He rubbed a hand over his shaved head and settled his mirrored shades back in place. "So, are you going to stand here chatting or are you going to the hospital?"

Gabe tucked his weapon back into place as the ambulance reached the highway, and with a roar of the high-powered engine sped off for the nearest emergency room. "I'm gone."

"I'll wait for the CSU to get here. Tell Sailor I'm thinking about her."

"Will do."

Ten minutes later, her purse held awkwardly in his hand, Gabe approached the desk at the ER. "Sailor Conyers? She was brought in by ambulance a little while ago."

"You family?" The woman behind the desk scratched the point of her pencil between two of her myriad corn rows and gave him a bland look. He wasn't getting any info out of her without anteing up himself.

"Yeah. Is she okay?"

"They took her straight on back. Any change in insurance or address info from her last time in the hospital?"

"I don't know."

"Sir, if you'll just give me the information, you can see her."

Gabe closed his eyes. He was not going to go nutso on this hospital woman. He needed to calm down, get the job done so he could get in to Sailor.

Okay, think, Gabe. He had Sailor's purse. Surely she had an insurance card and her driver's license would have her address on it. He dug through Sailor's information and handed it over.

After infinite typing and humming, the woman finally handed them back to him. "Yep, it looks like all the information is the same."

Gabe slid the cards back into place in Sailor's wallet.

"Right. Can I see Sailor now?"

"They took her back to Curtain Two."

Gabe hit the doors that led to the ER area at a full stride and headed straight for the desk. "Sailor Conyers?"

The nurse held the phone to her ear with her shoulder, a chart in one hand. She didn't look up, just held up the other hand to signal him to wait.

He stood at the desk, clenching and unclenching his fists, trying to ignore the universal industrial food smell from the cafeteria around the corner and the sounds coming from the various curtained areas. The beeps and whirs and moans all reminded him how little control he actually had. Tapping the counter, he tried to get the nurse's attention, but she steadfastly ignored him.

He couldn't wait anymore. Every second was another replay of the moment he spotted Sailor with blood pouring down her face. He'd thought—God help him, he'd thought that she'd been shot in the head. It had taken three long heart-stopping minutes for him to get his shirt off and wipe enough of the blood away to understand it was a cut where the canoe had struck her head. And then he'd had a new worry—head injury.

Surely Curtain Two had to be labeled? He just wanted to see those beautiful green eyes look into his.

A hand on his arm stalled him as he reached for a curtain. Another nurse that he immediately dubbed the "nice nurse" said, "You're Sailor Conyers's family?"

"Yes. Where is she? Can I see her?"

"They've taken her for a CT scan."

His heart dropped. "Why? Is there something wrong?"

"Usually with her kind of injury it's just a precaution, but I can't tell you any specifics. The doctor will be back in a few minutes. You can talk to him. In the meantime, have a seat, Mr. Conyers." She handed Gabe a manila envelope. "Your wife's things."

He didn't correct her—but he couldn't help but think what if these years had been different. Sailor *would* have been his wife.

But then maybe he wouldn't have fought in Africa alongside his friend Kitengi and a hundred others along the way—and he wouldn't have found the faith that had sustained him through some of the worst times of his life, that had called him home to finish the job his parents had started.

Maybe things worked out the way they were meant to. And in that case, he couldn't help wondering what he was doing here now. Maybe just protecting her was enough. Even with Cruse around, he had unique skills…and yeah, he had to believe God wanted them to resolve the past.

Steadier now, Gabe sat in the thinly padded, hideously orange chair just inside the curtained area, turning the manila envelope in his hands. The bumpy contents poked through the plain gold paper. He looked down the hall. No Sailor or doctor in sight. He opened the flap and poured the contents into his hand. Sailor's slim gold watch, and a long chain with a beat-up ring dangling at the end.

Gabe closed his fist around the ring he'd given her in high school, the match to the one in his pocket. The thing had only cost him about a dollar and a half. But it had meant something to Sailor for her to hold on to it for all these years. And there was more there than she was telling him.

He blew out a shaky breath.

Yeah, he was steady. He needed to get himself together. Needed to stop letting his emotions—about the past, about Sailor—get in his way and start thinking like a cop.

What did it all mean?

An attempt on Sailor's life, a break-in at her house. If Charlie's murderer was really gunning for her, this would have been a second miss. Could he be that lucky and the perps that inept? Not likely.

Was this related to Charlie's murder or did this have to do with Sailor's past? He still didn't have a solid clue, but he would find out. Climbing to his feet, he took one last long look down the hall, searching for those green eyes. But Sailor didn't have time for him to hang around, acting the lovesick fool. She needed him to think, to act like the expert he was. He strode down the hall.

He may not have many facts yet, but he knew one for certain. Sailor was in danger. And his protection alone wasn't going to be enough.

Crisp white sheets and the absence of color were the first things she noticed when she woke up in the hospital room. The second thing was the ferocious headache. The third thing was Maria Fuentes, laptop on her knees, an open box of chocolates on the desk beside her.

Sailor cleared her throat, licking dry lips as Maria lifted her eyes from the computer screen. "Hey, sleepy-head, it's about time you woke up." She slid to her feet and poured Sailor a glass of water.

Groping for the controls and finding them, Sailor cranked herself up a few feet so she could sip out of the cup. "Hey, yourself. What are you doing here?"

"Gabe wanted someone he trusted to stay with you while he's working."

Gabe hadn't said anything about going to work, but then she hadn't really given him a chance. She didn't think. Fuzzy-brained, she tried to remember back. She remembered going for a walk.

"Hey…hey, Sailor. You okay?" Maria asked, brow furrowed, one springy curl sticking to her cheek.

Was she okay? The doctors in the ER had said she was after they'd put seven stitches in her forehead. She drew some water from the straw in her glass. She squeezed her eyes shut. But since that hurt, she pressed her fingers over them instead. But that pulled the IV in her hand. She couldn't get comfortable.

She *hated* hospitals. But all things considered, technically, she guessed, she was okay. "I'm fine, Maria, thanks."

"Can I get you anything? I bet you'd like a Coke instead of water." Maria's dark eyes were filled with genuine concern.

"I'd love a Coke."

She let her head lie back against the pillows as Maria slid out the half-open door to the hall. The Coke would taste good, but Sailor desperately needed a few minutes alone to get herself together. She looked out the window. The sky was azure-blue again—typical of this time of year on the Florida coast. October and November were her favorite months to be out on the water. She'd give just about anything to be out there right now—in the wide-open seas—no people, no questions, just her and her fishing pole, soaking up the sun, instead of in this room, with these memories.

The last time she'd been in the hospital, she'd had a baby. The ache of it was as real as if it had been yesterday instead of more than seven years ago. Every emotion came flooding back…the indecision, the hope, and most of all, the crazy love. Despite everything, she'd loved that little baby so much.

Carts rattled by in the hall. She glanced at the half-open door, expecting to see Maria. Instead, Gabe filled the doorway. As she stared, Gabe turned his head and his warm brown eyes locked on hers. He nodded as if he'd been waiting just for that moment, then turned and walked away.

She closed her eyes, resting for a second, the murmur of quiet voices in the hall reminding her she was in a place of healing. She'd healed once. If he walked away, could she be strong enough to fill the hole he left in her life?

The part of her that still remembered the teenager she'd held hands with in the movie theater and under the table at McGuire's wanted to test the water and see. She believed in second chances; how could she not? But it was too late. Too much had happened between then and now. What she and Gabe had was over a long time ago, but with God's help, maybe they could be friends.

Gabe strode down the hall and around the corner, just in time to run into Cruse Conyers's fist. The punch knocked him back, but he didn't go down. And since he figured he probably deserved it, he didn't hit back.

Instead he gingerly rubbed the ache in his jaw. "She's fine. A headache and a few stitches, but there's no permanent damage."

"You're one lucky son of a gun. If my sister had been…"

"If Sailor had been hurt worse, I'd have been lining up to let you kick me to the curb. I let my guard down and I let you down, too. Sir."

Cruse took his measure, those cold green eyes a little intimidating, even for Gabe, who'd spent time in some extremely scary places. "Why is she alone now?"

"She's not. Maria Fuentes is with her. I figured someone she knows and trusts would be better than a stranger." He paused. "Better than me."

Cruse relaxed almost imperceptibly. "Where are you going?"

"I wanted to check out the security on this floor." He'd seen her. He'd looked into her eyes. He could get on with the business of protecting her.

Cruse silently walked the length of the hall with him, stopping to point at a security camera in the corner of the hall by the stairwell entrance. "What's going on with you and my sister?"

Gabe noted the camera. "It's been over with Sailor for a long time."

"Do you think I can't tell you're lying? I've been at this business a lot longer than you have."

Gabe stopped in the middle of the hall. That statement may or may not be true, considering his former profession, but he wasn't going to argue with his boss. "Okay. We planned to elope on a whim at seventeen, after…well, after. Only it wasn't a whim for me. How's that for the biggest cosmic joke?"

"I don't think it was a whim for her, either." Cruse walked to the camera in the corner at the left near the visitor's waiting area, eyeballed the angle and adjusted it a touch.

Gabe ignored Sailor's brother and his interfering. "Regardless of what it was then, it's not about that now. She needs protection. This business is ugly. To count it up, she's witnessed a murder up close and personal, barely missed surprising an intruder in her home, and been shot at."

Cruse's jaw bunched. "You don't have to be the one protecting her, not now."

Gabe scrubbed a weary hand through his hair. "I keep thinking, how many times did President Ngundi count on my detail to keep him safe? *I'm* an expert in personal protection. Not that it did her a lot of good this afternoon."

While Cruse adjusted the angle on the other camera, Gabe walked to the wide windows where he could see Pensacola Bay in the distance. The view was usually calming. Not today.

Anger was easier to deal with than hurt. And he'd held on to the fact that she'd walked away from their relationship. Being close to her these few days had undermined that anger more quickly than a hurricane could undermine the foundations of a building built on beach sand. The hurt, not so easily dismissed.

"Maybe you're a little distracted?"

Gabe turned from the window to face Cruse. He wasn't admitting anything. "It's going to take all of us to protect her."

Cruse's green eyes, so much like Sailor's, narrowed on Gabe. "Maybe you should back away."

Gabe's first instinct was to say "fine." But he wouldn't be the one to walk, not when he would be proving her right. Not when she was still in danger.

"I'd like to stay involved." He couldn't push, or Cruse would back him off faster than he could say "stand down, soldier."

When his boss finally nodded, Gabe expected relief. Instead, he had a sneaking suspicion the lieutenant had engineered this to come out exactly the way he wanted.

Cruse opened the door to the stairs. "I can't be with her 24/7, but you can. I'm clearing it. We're going to take care of her. We'll have contingency plans for our contingency plans."

"Yes, sir." Good protection meant countless hours of sheer boredom, but there were always those unplanned for moments of stark terror. And it was those moments that Gabe hated.

As Cruse disappeared down the stairwell, Gabe continued checking the doors and cameras. There wasn't a bodyguard in the world that could protect a client from every possible threat. It just wasn't possible. But in Africa he'd built a reputation on being the best. He'd staked his life on it.

Now he was staking Sailor's.

SIX

Gabe walked softly through the darkened halls of the hospital, still noisy with the soft beeps and whirs of equipment and the bustle of the staff even at this hour. He'd never understand how people were supposed to heal when they were being awakened all night long to have blood drawn or their pressure checked.

Reaching Sailor's room, he cracked the door, crooked a finger at Maria. When she slid into the hall, he tossed her the keys to his vehicle. "I'll take it from here."

The forensic specialist—who also happened to be extremely handy with a computer—arched a slender eyebrow, but kept her opinions to herself as she grabbed her shoulder bag and left.

Gabe sat in the chair Maria had vacated and took a look at the video she'd been watching from her sophisticated laptop. She'd managed to tap into the security feed and could keep an eye on the entire floor while keeping a close watch on Sailor.

He picked up one of her chocolates. Godiva. She must've done a favor for someone. Chocolate was her payment of choice. Maria did a lot of favors.

He tossed the rich candy back on the pile and slid the seat closer to the bed. He'd tried to stay away. He'd even meant to. Obviously being with him caused her pain. But he'd let her go twice, and twice she'd been harmed. He wasn't leaving her, not until he had a chance to see for himself that she was truly okay.

Her bare hand lay curled on the white sheet. At one time, he'd wanted nothing more than to see his ring on that finger. Now, he just wanted to see her survive this threat. He slid his hand under hers, reassured by the warmth.

She stirred, opened her eyes, looked steadily into his. No surprise, just welcome. "Hi."

"Hi, babe. You gave me a scare, you know." That moment when she lay still and silent would be forever seared into his brain.

"You're not going to fuss at me for running away from you?"

She surprised him by coming straight to the point. Slowly, he chose his words. "I think…seeing each other again is hard, on both of us."

Sailor smiled, a soft, sad curve of the lips. "Do you remember when we were in school, sometimes you used to come to my window at night so we could talk? That was before the days of cell phones."

"Your mom never could figure out why you talked to yourself so much." Gabe chuckled at the memory.

Mindful of her physical space, he didn't want to startle her. He knew she still bore emotional scars from enduring a rape, he just didn't know how deep those scars were. Easing a hip onto the edge of her bed, he waited for her to scoot over. A brief hesitation, and she did. He heard her swallow.

He played with the ends of her hair. "I still don't know how my parents never found out."

She laughed softly. "You'd sneak back through the woods before daylight. It's a miracle you didn't get snakebit."

It was a miracle he didn't get shot or beat up. Theirs had not been a nice neighborhood for kids to go tramping around after dark, especially a scared private-school kid, whose parents brought him into the hood to minister.

Sailor ran a finger along the edge of the industrial sheet on her hospital bed. "Do you remember Mrs. Cowan? She lived about three houses down from us."

"Kind of. What about her?"

"She was so sweet. When I was twelve, I used to go over in the afternoons to help her with her three-year-old twins. But really I went there because Mrs. Cowan made cookies and sometimes she let me play in her makeup. I really missed her when they moved away."

"What made you think about that?"

"There've been so many goodbyes, Gabe. I'm just not sure that I can survive another loss."

His free hand skimmed the curve of her neck. She sighed and tilted her face to his. "What's going on here, Gabe?"

"I don't know, Say-say."

She smirked at his use of her childhood nickname.

"I keep trying to stay away. And something keeps bringing me back to you."

Her eyes were full of everything that turned inside her. He knew because he felt the same way. He leaned forward—not much, just enough to brush his lips over her. The sensation rocked him.

Voices called in the hall. Gabe ignored them. A baby cried. Gabe ignored it. Nothing could keep him from this moment with Sailor.

Who had frozen in his arms.

Outside in the hall, that baby screamed. Gabe placed a kiss at Sailor's hairline. "You okay?"

She looked stricken. "What?"

Sailor rubbed a hand over her eyes as if rubbing away a bad dream. "Oh, yeah, I'm fine. Just really tired."

"I know you must be." But two seconds ago, she'd been relaxed in his arms. Something had startled her, but what? He slid into the chair beside the bed, but he maintained his hold on her hand. He wasn't quite ready to give up that fragile connection to her. "Just lay your head down and rest, Sailor. I'm not going to leave you."

Sailor hesitated, but then let her head drift back on the pillow. A few minutes passed and he heard her sleepy voice. "I missed you, Gabe."

He closed his eyes. What could he say? That she'd left a Grand Canyon–size hole in his life that he'd never been able to fill? That he'd dated women all over the world and not one—not one—had ever come close to making him feel what she did? That he didn't know if he'd ever be able to repair the damage she'd done to his heart?

Finally, he settled for the truth. "Yeah, I missed you, too, Sailor."

The early-morning sunlight streamed in the hall windows. The plush carpet in the law firm muted their footsteps. It didn't mute the fear, taking the form of butterflies tap-dancing in her belly. The hyper-vigilance of her two warriors didn't help.

Sailor looked up at Gabe, trying to maintain her footing while being nearly dragged along by her two self-appointed bodyguards. "Is this really necessary?"

He tipped a nod at her brother. "Ask him."

"Yes, it's necessary, if you want to go to the lawyer's office. I'm half-tempted to shut you up in a safe house as it is. Now be quiet, so I can hear over the earpiece." Her brother hauled her closer to him, and if possible, moved even faster, Gabe keeping pace on the other side.

According to the phone message left by T. Bradley Jones, the attorney handling Charlie's estate, everything in Charlie's will was ironclad, and the whole process would be expedited according to Charlie's wishes. As they reached the door to his private office, Maria came sliding out, her wild curls tamed into a relatively neat bun at the nape of her neck.

"We're clear." She took a post right outside the door, having insisted on joining Sailor's cadre of protectors on her day off. Sailor had no doubt that her slim, black suit hid more than one weapon. They'd taken target practice together at the range a few times. Maria was cold and deadly with her 9 mm.

Feeling slightly better, Sailor pushed the door open farther.

Gabe didn't release her elbow. Instead, he leaned in. "Want me to go in with you?"

It meant something that he'd ask. And since he did, she could say no and mean it. "I'll be all right."

The rich, dark paneling in T. Bradley's office did nothing to lessen the feeling of falling down a rabbit hole into someone else's life. Ken Banks, stoic in his black three-piece, sat across from Sailor. Layla clutched his hand with a white-knuckled grip, dressed in ladylike pearls and an olive-green suit.

Sailor shifted in her seat.

Finally, the door opened and the lawyer, a slightly hunched man in his mid-forties, strode to his desk. He threw several manila envelopes on his desk. "Mr. Banks asked that this be very simple, so I will follow his wishes to the T. There are three and only three bequests. I'm to read them out loud and there will be no discussion. Since Mr. Banks is no longer with us, there is no recourse for his decisions. Are we clear?"

Sailor gritted her teeth, the tension in this office so thick one of her commercial knives wouldn't cut it.

"Okay, so. First, Ms. Grady, Mr. Banks leaves his boat and his half of the partnership in the charter business to you."

Layla trembled out four rapid blinks, tears sliding like tiny jewels down her cheeks. She squeezed Ken's hand again and he pulled it away from her with an impatient shrug. To cover, Layla reached for the manila envelope that the lawyer held out to her and placed it on her lap, smoothing it the way one would a baby blanket or a handkerchief.

The lawyer turned back to the small crowd. "Ms. Conyers."

She held her breath. It had to be something small, just a token. Charlie had lived on his boat. The only other thing of value was the business.

"Mr. Banks left you two percent of the coffee shop, Sip This, bringing your total percent of ownership to fifty-one percent."

"What?" Ken Banks exploded to his feet. "He left her with controlling interest?"

Sailor sat in total shock. Why would Charlie do that? That two percent made a lot of difference in the balance of power.

T. Bradley Jones's voice cracked through the room. "Mr. Banks, control yourself. In addition, Ms. Conyers, the contents of this envelope were being held for you. Mr. Banks, the remaining percentage of the coffee shop Sip This, all other properties, interests and accounts, revert to you as his sole surviving relative."

Almost as quickly as it had erupted, Kenny's anger deflated, leaving him white and shaking, mumbling to Layla. She shushed him quietly.

The lawyer leaned over the desk to hand Sailor and Ken their envelopes and sat back down in the chair. "Please open your envelopes, verify the contents, and sign." He took three pristine pieces of paper and laid them precisely in a row in the front of his desk.

Layla peeled pack the flap on hers. "It's a letter." Her eyes welled again, but this time she swallowed the tears back as she reached for the lawyer's pen to sign.

A heavy knot of grief sat in Sailor's chest. She would've given anything not to do this—to have Charlie back instead of the coffee shop. She peeled the flap of her manila envelope, prepared to see another one inside. Instead, a small but heavy envelope thumped onto her lap.

"I think it's a key to a safety-deposit box," she said, hearing the question in her own voice. She hated this weird parody of Christmas morning, opening presents one person at a time, waiting to see what the other received. Instead of joyful anticipation, there was only extreme stress and the constant unbearable sorrow.

She signed the document the lawyer pushed forward to her.

"There will be additional documents regarding the coffee shop when the estate clears probate, of course."

"Of course."

Kenny stalked his way to the desk to sign that he'd received his letter—the only thing in his envelope—and the lawyer hurried across the room to hold the door open for them.

Sailor started out the door behind the others and collided with a hard chest. Gabe.

His deep voice rumbled across her ear as he leaned in. "Your brother got called out. Maria's getting the car for us."

She didn't want to feel anything for him. For so long, she'd thought that she had put the painful past behind her. Like it or not, Gabe represented that part of her life. But there was so much of everything between them, so much that still hadn't been said.

Maybe through Gabe's presence here, now, God was teaching her that she needed to deal with it, before something happened to her and, like Charlie, she left other people dealing with the consequences.

She looked up and her eyes collided with his. Her breath caught. He held her still in the doorway of the lawyer's office, his eyes inscrutable as he studied hers. The tap-dancing butterflies back in her stomach now had nothing to do with being afraid.

Abruptly, he broke the contact. "Time to go."

As he rushed her down the hall, she couldn't help

feeling she'd gotten caught up in someone else's tide, the current moving her swiftly in directions she wasn't sure she wanted to go and she didn't even know how she got here.

She'd always felt safe with Gabe. From the very first time she'd crashed into his hiding place under the magnolia tree at ten years old, to the last full-of-anticipation kiss.

But now, being with Gabe made her uncertain. He pushed her emotionally and demanded that she give in return. She just wasn't sure she had it in her to give what he was asking.

Gabe didn't speak as they took a different set of stairs from the one they had while coming up. At the car, Gabe opened the back door for Sailor, sliding into the seat beside her.

"Where to, Sailor?" His voice was terse.

For the first time in a long time, she didn't have a single idea. But she wouldn't let the questions win.

She refused to be a victim.

She held up the safety-deposit key. "First National Bank. Maybe we'll finally get some answers."

"The sooner we get into that safety-deposit box, the better." Gabe met Sailor's eyes as they pushed through the doors of the bank, Maria watching their six. "How's your head holding up?"

Her brow furrowed. "It's okay."

"Does it hurt?" They couldn't push her too hard. The doctors had been adamant that she take it easy. The CT scan hadn't shown an injury, but that didn't always mean one wouldn't show up later.

"No." She reached to rub her forehead but let her hand drop. "Really, I'm fine."

"We can put this off until tomorrow, Sailor." Gabe scanned the room.

"I want to get it over with." She relaxed, yet her fist stayed clenched tight, as if ready to fight at any moment.

She'd held up today, injured or not. She was hurting and exhausted now, though, and the sooner they were through this and he could put her to bed in his guest room, the better.

If they didn't need information so badly, he'd be the first to suggest they wait until she was stronger. Miss Independent probably wouldn't go for it even then.

She spoke to a bank officer, showing him the key and her ID. Within minutes, they were in the vault, gray walls of safety-deposit boxes stretched out on both sides at least ten feet.

The banker, with a questioning glance at Gabe, opened one of the larger bottom drawers and placed it in front of Sailor.

"Go ahead, Sailor, take a look." Gabe nudged the box closer to her.

She raised steady sea-green eyes to meet Gabe's and opened the lid. Old photos scattered the top.

Gabe laid those on the table. There was a letter addressed to Sailor. Then, a set of CD-ROMs labeled Bookkeeping Records.

Sailor nudged the CDs closer to Gabe, a confused look on her face. Last week's dates. Of course they couldn't be lucky enough to have old books. Sailor kept the current records on her laptop and stored backup disks in the safe, so that meant—

Charlie had been keeping a second set.

She opened her mouth to speak, but Gabe shook his head. *Not here.*

It looked like Charlie Banks had been cheating somebody. The question was, who?

"Open the letter and read what it says."

She slid her finger under the loosely glued flap of the envelope and pulled out a single sheet of notepaper. Her face scrunched into a frown.

Gabe forced himself to sit motionless, a skill achieved after long years of combat, endless waiting in the desert for something to happen.

Two long minutes passed. She looked up. "Basically? 'I'm sorry.'"

Sailor hadn't known her mentor was knee-deep in quicksand and going down fast. It was just a guess, but with that second set of books, and a murder with no one to point a finger at, Gabe figured Charlie had been laundering money. And dirty money equaled big-time danger.

With the contents of the box under one arm, Gabe led Sailor through the bank. It was up to Gabe to make sure that Sailor didn't get sucked into the same mire that had killed Charlie.

Maria waited by the front door. "All quiet. I don't think we were followed."

Gabe knew they weren't followed. There hadn't been a single sign of a tail. So why did he have that tingle on the back of his neck?

He pushed out the front door in front of Sailor, scanning the trees, the adjacent parking lot and the building across the street, a high-rise of doctors' offices. Nothing.

Gabe tucked Sailor into the back, Maria sliding in on the other side. As he jumped into the driver's seat, he met Maria's eyes in the rearview mirror. She shrugged and scanned the parking lot again—jumpy, but like him, unable to figure why.

Nerves jangled up his spine, the hair prickle turning to quick alarm. He needed to get Sailor out of here. He turned the key in the ignition. It clicked.

No way. Today was not the day they died. He threw open the door. Maria started shouting. Jerking the back door open, he hauled Sailor out. *"Run."*

Dragging her by the hand, he threw his body over a low wall, bringing Sailor with him to land on top, cushioning her fall. He rolled over to protect her with his body as a fireball of heat and debris shot over them, shaking the city block.

Pieces of the department-issued sedan rained down.

Sailor lifted her head, her eyes wide and terrified. "What happened? Where's Maria?"

"Running the other way. She should be fine." *God, please let her be fine.* He let his forehead drop to touch Sailor's. "That was close."

Sirens sounded in the distance as he pulled Sailor closer to his chest. It could've been her. He could have lost her. If she'd stopped to reach for her purse, she might still have been in the car.

He couldn't stop the hoarse sigh of relief, which told him the state of his heart was more precarious than he'd thought. He'd been without her for eight years and would've bet his favorite signed baseball that he could get two inches from her and still walk away. Coming face-to-face with losing her permanently twice in such a short time had shocked him into a little reality.

"Are you okay?" Her eyes searched his and the tender concern he saw there was as much a gift as a surprise.

"You're going to rip me to shreds again, aren't you, Sailor?" He couldn't turn away from her any more than he could turn his back on his duty. *Duty.* He needed to get his head on straight and start thinking like a cop.

She didn't answer, just spread her fingers on his chest where his heart beat triple-time.

Her eyes met his. "Gabe, what about the CDs?"

He reached underneath her and pulled out the huge envelope full of the contents of Charlie Banks's safety-deposit box. "Someone wanted these gone badly enough to try to blow us into eternity. Now we just need to figure out who."

Sailor didn't know what she'd expected from Gabe's home, but this wasn't it. His condo sat right smack on the spot that his mom and dad's shelter had been, but instead of the sprawling fellowship hall and dormitories, there were tiny houses, painted like beach houses with pretty streetlights and sidewalks. "I can't believe this is our old neighborhood."

Gabe smiled as he fingered numbers into a security pad. "It's pretty weird being back here, but it's fitting somehow."

Maria rubbed the back of her hand against a dirty scrape on her cheekbone. "Dibs on the shower."

"Upstairs." Gabe motioned Sailor farther inside as Maria started up. "The neighborhood is slowly being rebuilt. It still has a ways to go before it's safe to live in, but I don't think anyone would look for you here. And if they were looking for me, they wouldn't find me. This place is under the radar."

Sailor wandered, touching things while Gabe built a fire—the frame of a subtly lit Nina Fritz watercolor, a bell jar of shells, the brass fittings from a sailboat. "Your place is beautiful."

He sat back on his heels, the kindling crackling and hissing in the fireplace. "I like it."

The firelight glinted off the silky golden brown of his hair and shadowed the grooves of his face, but she saw a slight curve of the lips as he settled beside her. He lowered his eyes, long golden-tipped lashes covering brown eyes that had always shown her too much of what he'd felt. The tip of his finger skimmed her bare arm and tingles ran to her toes.

He looked at her then and what she saw in his eyes made her breath absolutely leave her body. She'd lived a careful life. He was a man who would put his body in front of a bullet for her. There was a fineness in him that had nothing to do with his physique.

She couldn't do this. She couldn't let herself fall under his spell again but she could be a friend. "We need to take care of your cuts."

"They're fine. I'm fine."

She jolted to her feet. "I'll find the first-aid kit and I'll be right back."

His head thunked back on the sofa cushion as she walked away. She took a deep breath. The cut on his face looked deep, and she could, at the very least, take care of him in that way.

In the bathroom, she found a tackle box with medical supplies. Her hands shook as she pulled out antibiotic ointment and bandages.

Gabe hadn't moved when she returned. Exhaustion was carved into his features.

She poured antiseptic onto a cotton ball. "Hang on, this is going to smart."

He sucked a sharp breath in as she dabbed the cleanser over the cut on his cheek.

"I'm sorry. I'm so sorry."

"It's no big deal, Sailor. If a few cuts on my back and face are my only injuries, I was lucky."

Because he'd put himself in harm's way, his back and arms caught the worst of the shards of metal hurtling through the air. She shuddered as she thought of how much worse it could have been but wasn't because he moved so fast to protect them both.

When she pressed the last bandage into place, she saw his shoulders relax a fraction. "All right, soldier. You're all patched up."

She leaned forward to drop a peck on his wounded cheek. Instead, he slid one hand into the hair at the base of her neck and pulled her in for a kiss. It wasn't the powerful, drugging kiss of infatuation she remembered as a teenager, but it was no less devastating for its gentleness.

She sighed and laid her head on his shoulder. He cuddled her close, and she let herself imagine, just for a minute, what it would have been like to be his for good.

When she looked at him, his eyes were dark with emotion before he shuttered them. "You should go to bed, Sailor."

They were both tired and emotionally overwhelmed, their defenses low. As hurt tried to worm its way in, she told herself the kiss had only been a reaction to the stress and adrenaline that had poured through them from a narrow escape. Gabe was right to pull away.

"There are three bedrooms upstairs. You'll take the middle one. Maria and I'll have the ones on either side." He hesitated. "You'll have to leave the door open."

Sailor started for the stairs that hugged the wall leading to the upstairs loft and bedrooms. At the base, she paused. All of the feelings from past and present were mixing up inside her and she didn't know if she could make him understand. She turned back, but his face was buried in his hands.

"Gabe."

He lifted his head. The firelight glowed warm on his face, but he looked so weary. She realized how heavy this burden he'd chosen to take on must weigh on his shoulders. The responsibility of keeping her safe, sure, but somehow so much more.

"I'm so sorry."

He held her eyes, but she was too far away to read them. Finally, he said, "I know, Sailor. Me, too."

She turned to walk away, taking the steps slowly. The bedroom was an escape, a cool, dark haven from so much pain and stress. He'd said to leave the door open, but she had to have privacy, had to be alone.

She was strong, but she'd had an unbelievable few days. Sailor pressed her fist to her mouth. The enemy stalking her seemed stronger and more determined. He'd *killed* her friend and tried to kill her twice.

Her safe life had turned into a terrifying horror

show—one that, even with Gabe on her side, she wasn't sure she could survive.

Maria traveled the distance from the stairs to the kitchen in her usual efficient manner, her hair wrapped in a towel. Pulling a glass from the cabinet, she jammed it under his ice dispenser. "Not that it's any of my business, but what are you thinking?"

Gabe walked to the kitchen island, braced his hands against the cool black granite. "I was just wondering that myself."

Maria popped the top on a Diet Coke. "Please be careful, Gabe. I don't want to see either one of you hurt again."

"The last thing I want to do is hurt Sailor." He brushed a nonexistent crumb off the shiny surface. "I spent so many years fighting for peace in other people's countries. I thought it was time to come home and make peace with my own past. It's harder than it should be."

She shook her head. "I don't think looking back is the way to find peace in the present."

"No. But in this case, it may be the way to catch a killer."

A sharp cry, abruptly muffled, sounded from upstairs. In that instant, Gabe went from guardian to warrior. Motioning to Maria, he took the stairs two at a time.

Sailor's door was closed. All the way closed. Pulling his weapon, he slid up the wall to the outside of Sailor's door, Maria edging quietly to the other side. He glanced at her, motioned for her to check out the other rooms.

Whipping open the door, he went in low. In seconds,

he knew that he could put the gun away. There was no danger here, but it didn't mean that Sailor didn't need him. The sheets twisted around her legs as she tossed and turned.

Maria appeared in the door. Gabe raised an eyebrow, a question on his face.

She backed away, shaking her head.

Gabe's heart hurt at the thought of what Sailor had been through, what must lurk in her nightmares. Sobs shuddered through her from somewhere deep inside, the sound cutting through him like a knife. The raw pain, the stark fear, wound through him, shredding his emotions, leaving him wide open. With hands deliberately gentle, he reached for her.

"No!" She clawed at his hands, hers like ice, as she scrambled away from him.

"Sailor, it's me, honey. It's Gabe. Shh—I'm not going to hurt you."

Wrenching back, her eyes were wide, but she didn't see him. She only saw the horrors that held her in their grasp and kept her away from him, away from safety and peace.

"I'm right here, baby. You're safe."

Lost in the dream, she dug her heels into the mattress, scrambling back until she could curl her knees into her chest. Easing beside her, he pulled her closer until she was cradled in his arms, his back against the headboard. The violent cries eased, but she shoved at his shoulder, pushing him away.

As he rocked, her hand relaxed, then fisted in his shirt. *Oh, my God, what has she been through?*

Tears streamed from her eyes now, but she didn't make a sound.

"Sailor, are you with me?"

Long pause. "Yeah. I'm okay."

She wasn't. It was obvious she wasn't okay, not by a long shot. He kissed her damp temple as she buried her face, moist from her tears, in the curve of his neck. He held it there with his hand stroking her hair, the other holding her against his chest.

When he was ten years old, she'd come stumbling and skidding into his hiding place, all long gangly legs, skinned-up knees and gigantic green eyes. He'd given her his heart then and he'd never gotten it back, that much was apparent. But what he felt then didn't compare to what he was starting to feel for the strong woman in his arms.

"How bad is it, Sailor? Do you dream like this every night?" *Please say no*. He couldn't bear to know she suffered like this every night.

"No. I haven't had one for a while. It's not always this bad." She trembled in the aftermath, a fine tremor running through her with every breath.

"Bad enough. Do you want some water?"

Her hand clenched tighter, his shirt pulling taut across his chest. "Don't go."

"I'm not going anywhere, honey. I promise."

She was in a mess. Assassins after her, people dying. The explosion today after everything else must have triggered the nightmares. A money trail from Charlie to something she really wasn't going to want to know.

But that wasn't the question. The question was, did he want her in his life? Or maybe a better question would be, after seeing her and being with her again, could he take his next breath *without* her in it?

He closed his eyes and held her as she drifted off. He didn't want to know.

Three hours later, at two in the morning, Gabe had a monster-size cup of coffee at his elbow and the contents of Charlie's safety-deposit box spread all over his kitchen table. Some clue had to exist—a way to find out why Sailor was being targeted, *if* Sailor had been targeted because of Charlie. He'd left her on top of the covers, curled around a pillow, the tracks of her tears obvious on her face, his hands clenched into fists desperate to punish the person who made her cry.

The financial records from Sip This were simple. Charlie was running big-time money through the coffee shop, nearly ten thousand dollars per day—just under the bank's requirement to report to the federal authorities. His note to Sailor was cryptic. He was sorry. But what was he sorry for?

He was getting the money from somewhere. And Gabe would bet that "somewhere" got him killed. Knowing that, Gabe could release some of his sense of culpability that Sailor had been injured, but that relief lasted for all of one gulp of coffee. Because, well, she was still in danger.

Gabe flipped a glance up the stairs. The door was still cracked open the way he'd left it, the room where Sailor slept still dark, all quiet. He lifted the second envelope that Charlie had left in the safety-deposit box and slid the paper out.

You're a daughter to me, Sailor, more of a child than my own. I'm sorry to leave this to you, but you're stronger than you know. I wish I'd been the man you thought I was. I do love you, sweetie, and I'm sorry. Charlie

Whatever.

His instincts told him that more of this mess went back to Charlie than they'd even suspected. He needed more information, which, if the strings he'd pulled came through, he should have by morning.

Gabe took a swig of his coffee and picked up the seven photographs. They were in color, but they were old, maybe from the early eighties, if the color and processing was any indication. He could take them to an expert for analysis if it came to that.

The setting was tropical, probably Caribbean, from the color of the water. There were two photos of boats with, Gabe guessed, a young Charlie standing on board with some other men. One on the front porch of a huge house, and one of him in the sugarcane fields. Maybe he worked sugarcane? There was a photo of an empty beach, and one of him wrapped around a girl on the wide veranda of…a resort?

Gabe grabbed the magnifying glass and held it over the photo. Three letters—*a-l-s*—showed on the wall behind them. Sandals? Had there been a Sandals resort in Jamaica that far back? And what would young kids have been doing at such a ritzy place?

He went back to the boat picture with the magnifying glass. Sure enough, when he looked closely, the home port on the stern of the charter boats was Montego Bay. Bingo.

Too many questions with too few answers, but Gabe had a feeling that Jamaica was the place to start finding them. He took shots of the photos with his Blackberry and e-mailed them to Joe and Cruse. If Joe could make contact with sources in Jamaica then maybe, just maybe, they'd find some of those answers. At the least, it was another string to pull.

Sailor could drop out of sight for a day or two until they had more information. Staying here would be the best option. No one knew where they were. She could stay here in complete safety.

Gabe took the stairs up two at a time. She wouldn't like having to take a leave from her business, but once he explained the situation to her, she'd see his point of view. She'd have to realize he knew what he was doing. After all, he was a professional.

Too bad he couldn't keep from deluding himself. This case was extremely personal.

Sailor's inner alarm clock roused her—wake time for her was four-thirty in the morning. The shower running in the bathroom adjacent to her room motivated her to roll out of bed and get moving. She stumbled down the stairs to the kitchen.

Gabe had obviously been awake for a while. He had papers and photos scattered all over the kitchen table, along with his laptop. She scanned the notes on the yellow legal pad. He'd apparently traced Charlie to Jamaica, if the name of that tiny Caribbean island circled a dozen times meant anything.

She opened a couple of cabinets until, above the coffeepot, she hit pay dirt. Coffee beans and tea bags. The mugs were neatly aligned in the next cabinet. After filling her cup and starting the microwave for two minutes, she pressed her fingers to her eyes. They felt bruised. *She* felt bruised.

The vestiges of her nightmare still hung in the edge of her imagination. Unfortunately, she had personal experience to prove that nightmares weren't all the stuff of dreams. Some were all too real.

But Gabe had been there last night to fight off the monsters, and that was a whole 'nother level of scary. When he left eight years ago, she had to pick up the pieces of her life and move on without him. Her choice, she knew, but depending on him again came with a new set of fears.

She snagged her mug from the microwave and dunked the tea bag into the steaming water. Routine helped. Her day started with checking for messages from her employees. Gabe's computer sat open on the table, so bringing it out of standby, she quickly logged onto her server and retrieved her e-mails. Three spam messages deleted, a few condolences…

Pop.

The report of the gunshot sent her scrambling for cover on her knees under the table. It cracked through the room twice more before she realized it was only a sound effect from the e-mail she had opened. Taking a deep breath, she rose from her hiding place to take a look at the e-mail. A picture of Gabe outside on the back porch of Sip This, so it couldn't have been taken more than a few days ago. His eyes were narrowed to scan the alley, and he had his cell phone to his ear.

As she watched, the shot sounded again and a black bullet hole appeared in Gabe's forehead. The color of the photo drained out one pixel at a time, leaving only garish cartoonlike bright red blood coursing down his face.

Bloodred words appeared one letter at a time. *"STOP OR HE'S NEXT."*

Her lungs seized, robbing her of air. When the gunshot cracked again, a breath whistled in. She slammed the screen down, looking wildly around the room. What should she do?

She had to get away from here. Whoever sent this e-mail knew enough to get her private e-mail address and had gotten close enough to Gabe to take this photo. He could as easily have taken a shot that day as a picture. What if Gabe died because of her?

Sailor slowed herself down. She needed to think—was she being stupid, walking away? No, she had to protect him now. She could tell Maria, but Maria would stop her, only putting them all in more danger. Shaking her head, she realized the best way—the only way—was on her own, the way she had always been. This time without Charlie as a safety net.

Pulling Gabe's notebook toward her, she scribbled a note, hoping against hope to stay his search, even for a few minutes' head start.

She started stuffing the papers, disks and photographs into her purse. Everything that would fit from the safety-deposit box. She could sort through it on the plane.

Gabe had made her leave her shoes by the back door, so she slid her feet in those. Now the hard part. The alarm. She'd watched Gabe disarm it, but she hadn't paid much attention. One chance to get it right, and if she blew it, she blew her one chance to protect Gabe from whoever was after her.

Not daring to breathe, she pressed the four numbers she thought she'd seen him press and waited for the alarm to blare. A second later, the screen changed and the light on the side went to green. Her breath whooshed out. She'd done it.

Snatching his keys from their hook beside the garage door and taking one quick glance back, she walked through the back door, away from safety. Away from Gabe.

No regrets. She was doing the only thing she could to protect Gabe. He may not understand at first. In fact, he'd be mad as all get out, but he'd come around. He'd know she'd protected him the only way she could.

Gabe oiled the garage doors regularly, so the gears on those things were pretty ridiculously quiet. But the grind of the door opening and closing seconds later was unmistakable. His heart rate picked up speed. He reached for his Glock and checked the load. Moving quickly and quietly on his bare feet, he checked Sailor's room. Bed empty.

He met a tousle-headed Maria in the hall, gun up and ready. He shook his head and motioned downstairs. He had multiple safeguards in place. Not one of them had been tripped.

Bad guys pretty much never came in through the garage, anyway. Too noisy. An open window, a jimmied door. All more quiet than rigging the garage door.

From the stairs he could see ninety percent of the downstairs. Empty. Gabe ran for the back door, hesitating briefly before he threw open the door to the garage and entered the room in one smooth motion.

The Hummer was gone. *She* was gone.

From the other end of the house he heard Maria shout, "We're clear."

He lowered his gun. Her mug sat by the kitchen sink, a teabag tag hanging over the side. The tea was way too strong to drink. He felt the cup. Still hot to touch. She hadn't been gone long. Why would she leave without a word?

He couldn't buy it. Something had happened to Sailor, something he'd missed. He made himself take his time as he cleared the garage, but inside his gut twisted.

"She's been taken, Maria."

"Back up, hotshot. She has a history of disappearing from your life. Let's look around before you jump to that conclusion."

The papers were missing. Obvious. What else? He ran back over what had been on the table when he left the room. Had he closed his laptop?

No, he'd been waiting for e-mail from his intelligence contacts regarding Charlie Banks.

His pad lay at an angle on top of his laptop. He saw the note, scribbled in pencil.

Gabe, I know that you're doing your best for me, but I can't be with you anymore. Please don't follow me. Sailor

He tossed the pad onto the table. Despite all the hardship of her life growing up, she'd made a successful life here. Why would she run? Why was running better than staying and facing what made you afraid? "Maybe it was staged to look like she left. Someone could have forced her to write a note."

Maria hesitated. "Maybe…"

Gabe opened the laptop. The machine whirred to life under his fingers.

Reflex had his weapon in his hand before he realized the gunshot was a sound effect. Struggling to stay detached, he studied the picture of himself as the color drained out of it, and the shocking red words appeared on the screen.

If he hadn't suspected already that the perp knew Sailor personally, he did now. She'd barely shown a reaction, at least a public one, when she'd been shot at. He and her brother and Maria, the other members of the force had closed rank around her and protected her. But whoever sent this e-mail knew the best way to isolate Sailor would be to threaten *someone else*.

He glanced at the key holder to make sure the keys were gone, but he already knew they would be. So she'd taken his Hummer. She'd also taken the papers. Would she go off on her own to investigate?

The old Sailor he used to know wouldn't have. The new Sailor? He couldn't be sure, but it was a pretty good bet that she'd go the distance to get life safely back the way she liked it.

But that made the chance of someone targeting her while she was on her own even greater, and the stakes even higher. He looked at Maria.

"I'll get the department to put a BOLO out for the Hummer." She had her phone in her hand, dialing.

"Can you check the airlines, see if she booked a flight?"

Maria shoved him aside, phone clamped under her ear, her fingers tapping furiously on the keyboard of his laptop as she hacked into the various databases.

He couldn't stay here, knowing Sailor was out there alone, in danger. Even knowing she'd left him— again—he had to make sure she was safe. "I'm going to look for her. Give me a call when you get something."

"Got it. She's booked on Delta flight 1208 leaving at 6:30 a.m. through Atlanta getting into Mo Bay at 12:30 p.m. She'll need her passport. Maybe you can catch her at her house?"

Gabe slammed the door behind him, cutting off her words. He fired up the Beach Police truck and wheeled out of his driveway onto the still-dark street.

So, the good news. He knew where Sailor was heading. The knot in the pit of his stomach eased but didn't disappear. Because now he had to get to her before the killers did.

SEVEN

Sailor clenched the steering wheel in a white-knuckled grip. The passport she needed to travel was just inside the door—the door of her dark house that had been ransacked by strangers just two days ago. The same strangers who had killed her friend Charlie.

What was she doing? She had to be brave. If she wanted to find out what was going on, she needed to follow the trail that Charlie had left. That meant Jamaica according to Gabe's notes. So she had to get out of the car.

She reached for the handle. A dark face appeared in the window. Sailor screamed, panic flooding her system. She fumbled for the keys, but her hands shook. She couldn't make them work, couldn't get away. She'd been so stupid to come here.

"Sailor! It's me. Open the door."

The words penetrated her panic. Gabe?

The fear receded, but adrenaline still coursed through her. She forced air into lungs that had seized up, warring emotions of relief and disappointment that she hadn't been able to get away coursing through her. Seconds later, Gabe slid into the passenger seat.

"Do you have any idea the kind of danger you put yourself in taking off like that?" His voice was low, but his fury came through loud and clear.

When she didn't speak, he reached for her hand and peeled her fingers one by one off the steering wheel. "I saw the e-mail, Sailor."

She stared out the window, not daring to look at him. "I watched one of my friends die this week, Gabe. Do you think I could survive if I had to watch you die, too? I had to leave."

"I understand why you thought you had to." His words were slow and careful. "But here's something else to consider. I'm a cop working a job. Whoever is stalking you knows I've been in on this every step of the way. Do you really think leaving will protect me?"

She stared at him, one trembling tear stuck in her bottom lashes. "I never thought—oh, Gabe, I'm so scared. The attack on me when I was seventeen, that was bad. This is worse. I don't know who is after me, or really even why. Right now I feel like my entire world is crumbling and there's not a safe place for me anymore."

"It's okay to be scared, Sailor. It's human nature, and a healthy dose of self-preservation."

"You're not."

"I've been there."

The dark cocooned around them, the secret-sharing coming back as naturally as his fingers twined with hers.

"Warfighters are highly trained operatives." He hesitated, his eyes narrowed against the memories. "And when I was being held by the rebel fighters, I spent my nights curled in a ball, with artillery and shells rattling in the distance, praying for daylight."

She tightened her fingers on his.

"Being brave has nothing to do with how scared you are. It has everything to do with facing what you're afraid of and doing the right thing."

Sailor looked at their fingers, curved together palm to palm. How could they look so right together? He said the right words, did the right things, and her heart wanted to believe. Her head told her that what she wanted wouldn't happen for her.

But when he pulled her close and wrapped his arms around her, she laid her head on his strong shoulder. Would it really hurt to depend on him? To be held, to be comforted, to be in his care just this once. Maybe it would give her the strength to do what she needed to do.

Sailor took a deep breath. "All my life I've tried to protect the people I—care about. I was cleaning my mother up and tucking her into bed when I was in elementary school. And after the rape—"

She cut herself off.

"After the rape, what?"

Sailor hesitated, the words she needed to say sticking in her throat. Because once he knew, what could he feel but more regret?

"Sailor, what are you keeping from me?" He could be angry, but he sounded baffled. And she had to remember that she hadn't lived through that time in a solo universe, no matter how alone she felt at the time. To understand, Gabe had to know what happened.

The fear faded, like the surf, sucking back into itself.

It would be back, just like the waves on the beach. But right now, she knew she had to do the right thing.

She took a deep breath. "I found out a month after the attack. My wounds and bruises had healed, mostly. I thought my insides were messed up, or maybe the trauma of it all caused my symptoms. It was…quite a shock, to hear I was pregnant."

"You were—" Gabe thought he'd put the past behind him, that it didn't have the power to hurt him anymore. But imagining Sailor alone, wounded, *pregnant*—it was a body blow he didn't even think of blocking. He didn't know what to say, but knew he needed to say something. "What—aah—what did you do?"

"Rationally, I knew that it wasn't my fault that I got pregnant, but I hated the man who attacked me and made me feel less than a person. I didn't want a child. But the first time I felt that baby move…Gabe, I knew she was a miracle—that God could make something amazing out of something so horrible. She deserved a chance to live." Her arms were crossed over the steering wheel, her posture defensive. Would he question her decision?

He tried, really tried, not to judge her for shutting him out. She'd been seventeen, afraid, making life-changing decisions. But she hadn't had to make them alone. "What did you do?"

"I'd been with my brother while I was healing, but I had to get a job, or I knew we wouldn't make it. Charlie took me in, gave me a place to live and a job. But more than that, he gave me my self-respect back. You know?"

"Sailor, did you ever think about letting me help you?"

She let her head drop to the steering wheel. Her voice, muffled by her crossed arms, still trembled with remembered pain.

"Yeah, I did." He almost missed it, she said it so softly.

"When?" He didn't want to believe her. If she had come to him, there was no way he would have ever let her go, not then.

When she lifted her head, he met her clear green gaze. Once again, she was telling the truth. "I just wanted to hear your voice, to hear you tell me it would be okay. I went to the mission shelter that your mom and dad ran, figuring they'd know how to find you. I hid across the street and watched your dad. He welcomed in the beggars and homeless off the street and into the shelter for a hot meal, clean clothes, a shower."

He let her talk. Eight years too late, she was filling him in on the events that had changed the course of his life.

Sailor drew her knees up, her legs long in the dark blue jeans. She wrapped her arms around them, as if perhaps by folding herself up she could protect some intrinsic part of herself that she'd kept closed off with this secret that she'd carried for so long.

"I realized that day, watching your dad, that I had become one of the very people that your father ministered to. Pregnant teenager, abused, broken. Your father would have taken me in without a single blink. *Into the shelter.*

"But into his life? Into his son's life? I only asked him for your address that day. He wouldn't give it to me. And he sure wouldn't have welcomed me into your life, a teenage mother pregnant with another man's child."

Gabe's fist shot out to slam into the dashboard and she jumped. "Did you think that mattered to me? *You* mattered."

He rolled the window down to let in the chilly, early-morning sea breeze. It didn't help to cool the simmering pot of emotions bubbling below the surface. Resentment, a little anger still, and so much regret. That he could have been there for Sailor and his father's choice had taken his own away from him.

"I know." Her hand was soft on his back, over the still-healing wounds from the jagged metal of the explosion at the bank.

Problem was, some wounds never healed. Like those that his father had made by having so much compassion for everyone else, and none when it really mattered. Wounds like the ones that Sailor had from a childhood of neglect, from a traumatic attack.

He shook as she touched him. "Oh, Gabe, don't you think I know you would have traded your future to take care of me and a baby that wasn't even yours? We could have made it, probably, but what kind of life would that have been? Two teenagers trying to raise a kid?"

"I didn't have the choice." The words were stark, the way the pain felt inside, ragged-edged and new again, hearing the real truth, finally, of why she left him. Why she sent that letter breaking things off for good.

He wanted to hold her, the frightened young girl that she'd been. But now she was a woman, pleading for his understanding. And the truth was she hadn't trusted him enough to give him the choice to stand by her.

He shook his head. "You didn't give me the choice, Sailor."

She turned him around to face her in the early-morning light. Her eyes were huge and luminous, dark emotion swimming in them. "Selfishly, I wanted to keep her. But, Gabe, I wasn't just protecting you by giving her up for adoption. I was protecting her, too. Giving her a chance that I didn't have, and a safe place to call home."

Gabe knew he didn't have all the answers. Even having found his way to God in a little thatch-roofed church in Africa, he could barely walk his own path, much less lead someone else, and he couldn't turn away from the lost look in her eyes.

She'd made a hugely brave decision, and she'd been carrying this around on her own for eight years. "You did a good thing for her. You made a really courageous decision, and I'm so proud of you."

He slid an arm around her, pulling her closer to him. For a God who used everything to His purpose, surely there was a reason he'd been brought into Sailor's life again, even if it was just for this moment of acceptance. He pulled her in to his chest and whispered in her hair, "I'll be your safe place, Sailor."

Gabe sprawled across the gleaming black countertop in the kitchen at Sip This. Sailor had wanted to work, bury herself in what she knew. He didn't argue, just stayed two steps behind her all morning as the customers poured in, business as usual.

This "unsub," as they called the unknown subject, tended to like a little distance, like the e-mail and the long-range gun. Even the bomb wasn't an up-close-and-personal-type kill. Gabe knew she'd be safer if he buried her in an unknown location, but cops would be in and out all day and he'd asked for extra eyes on the coffee shop and surrounding property.

He'd gotten a total of two hours of rest, and after the conversation in the car felt a little soul-battered. Sailor had whipped her black apron around her and never hesitated, her hands flying as she mixed ingredients.

"Blueberries."

"What?"

"I need blueberries from the walk-in. Can you get them?" She waggled fingers coated with dough for scones. "I'm a little sticky here."

He peeled himself from the stool. "Did Charlie ever mention spending time in Jamaica?"

"No. I knew he did some time charter fishing on some big boats in the Caribbean—it's where he learned, but he didn't tell stories about those times, not ever."

Gabe's BlackBerry beeped at him. He pulled it out, checked the message, the cooler blowing cold dry air in his face. "If the contacts in Jamaica come through, we could find a starting place for tracing his life before he was a barista in Sea Breeze, Florida."

"Why didn't you just Google him?"

"I did. So did an investigator I contacted. He just e-mailed." Gabe turned the BlackBerry around so she could read the screen. "We've checked every database we could think of. Your friend didn't exist before 1985."

"What?" She grabbed Gabe's shoulder with a doughy hand.

Charlie—her friend, her father figure, the one person she'd thought she could count on—had lied. About everything.

Gabe slid the berries across the counter. "We dug up a Charles Banks born in Chicago in 1949. He died in 1954. Taking the name and stats of a deceased person is the most common way of assuming a false identity. I'm sorry, Sailor."

She stood in front of him, her very presence reminding him how far she'd come, how much she'd *overcome*. She deserved an answer, before she broke.

The back door slammed open and Gabe's partner strode through it. In blue jeans, a brown leather bomber jacket, Joe's mirrored sunglasses were in place, even at ten in the morning.

"Hi, Joe. What can I get for you?" Sailor slid the pan of scones into the oven and wiped her hands on her apron.

"Loads of caffeine, loads of sugar."

"Coming right up." Sailor's soft laugh, despite the pain he knew she felt, sent a spear of pain through Gabe's chest. She was so outrageously brave.

He'd like to avoid the questions and save her more grief, but she needed to know. They both needed to know what her boss had been up to. Every scrap of information led them closer to an answer to who was after Sailor and why. They couldn't afford to wait any longer. "All right, Joe. Let's have it."

"I had to bribe one of the department's computer experts to get up at three forty-five this morning to look this stuff up. Sorry, Sailor, but I promised he'd get free coffee for a month."

"Joe." Gabe warned with his tone.

"We traced one of the photos to a historic sugar plantation owned by a Franklin Peters. Mr. Peters is a traditional kind of guy, about eighty, I'd guess. I faxed him the picture and he hedged. He said he recognized the people but no names. I have to tell you though, I had a feeling he knew more. He sounded really shook up when he found out that Charlie Banks had been murdered."

"That's it?"

"Give me some credit. I called back and talked to the butler who answered the phone. He recognized our boy and gave him a name—Michael Trainer."

"What else?"

"Patience, Gabe, I'm getting to it. Trainer was apparently like a son to old Mr. Peters, but he started hanging out with the rich kids vacationing at the resort—the wrong crowd, especially for Michael Trainer. He fell in love with a girl and she played him for a fool."

"In what way?" Sailor asked, as she reached behind her to open the oven door. The sweet, fresh aroma of baking scones filled the kitchen.

"The story is that this girl convinced Trainer that her boyfriend was beating her up. One night at the resort, he found them together. Thinking she was in danger, he killed the boyfriend. The butler seemed to think that she set him up."

Joe took off his sunglasses, rubbed at a nonexistent spot, and put them back in place. "He didn't want to tell me the rest of the story, but I convinced him. Finally he spilled it. They got Trainer out of the country on one of the old guy's charter boats, and Peters gave Trainer what he needed to start over."

He turned to Sailor. "Apparently everyone at Good

Hope plantation agreed that your friend was something special."

Sailor paled, and she wobbled on her feet.

"Sailor?" Gabe reached for her, but she pulled away. "It might not even be the same person. That was a long time ago."

She dug something out of the pocket of her black pants and tossed it on the counter. "I've been carrying this picture of Charlie around. It was one of his favorites of the two of us."

Gabe drew it toward him to take a closer look. Sailor and Charlie stood in the stern of a large boat, both holding huge fish, both with silly grins on their faces. But what caught his eye was the name on the boat. *The Good Hope*.

He raised his eyes to meet Sailor's troubled green ones.

She nodded. "I'm pretty sure they're the same person. And that means my mentor…the closest thing I've ever had to a father was a fugitive and possibly a murderer."

Work crept by as Sailor tried to put a smile on her face and put out of her mind the fact that Charlie had never been what he seemed. Even the lull between the morning breakfast crowd and the afternoon caffeine junkies, a time she usually had no trouble filling, dragged. She sighed and squirted the glass pastry cabinet with cleaner.

A large, warm hand closed over hers, stilling the frantic motion. "Sailor, you've wiped that four times." Compassion filled Gabe's eyes. "Erasing the smudges on that glass isn't going to erase the hurt from Charlie lying to you."

She squirmed, pulling her hand from his grip. "I realize that. And I understand there are bigger issues here. I just can't seem to get my mind around them."

Instead of reaching for her hand, he reached for her, enfolding her in his arms. She leaned into him, and as she relaxed, his arms closed even more tightly around her. "It's going to be okay."

"Will it? It won't ever be the same." Tears threatened and she blinked them back. "Believe it or not, despite everything I know now, I really miss him."

He skimmed a finger down her cheek. "I know you do, sweetheart. And you have every right to grieve. Charlie cared about you. That part wasn't a lie."

It would be so easy to depend on Gabe the way she once had, but she'd come way too far to ever be that dependent on another person. She didn't need to be rescued. Even if she wanted to be.

Footsteps pounded down the hall, and Chloe's beanie-covered head appeared in the doorway. "Oops, sorry."

Sailor disengaged from Gabe's arms, her face heating. "Hey, Chloe. What's up?"

"I just wanted to talk to you about the computer program you use to keep track of stuff you've ordered. It's really archaic."

"If you want to set up something—for test purposes only—we'll give it a trial run. I could definitely use a program that would make life less complicated."

The teen she'd taken in scratched her head through the wool cap, a mutinous expression appearing on her face. "I'm not going to mess anything up, Sailor."

"I trust you." She grabbed the arm of Chloe's black hoodie as the teenager turned to run. "Chloe. I trust you. But I have to be able to keep track of inventory. The old program has to work until a new one is up and running."

Chloe shrugged off Sailor's hand but relaxed a fraction. "Okay, fine."

"The most current files are in my laptop on my desk at home."

She watched Chloe tromp out the back door in her heavy combat boots. When Sailor turned back to Gabe, she could easily read the expression on his face.

"Yes, Gabe, I know it's risky to let her into the computer. But everything important is backed up and password protected."

"I didn't say anything, but now that I think about it, I need to check her out. It's pretty convenient her showing up here when she did."

She looked down at the cleaning rag still in her hands. "She reminds me so much of me when Charlie took me in, taught me to be someone."

Gabe shook his head, and walked behind the counter to grab a cup. "False logic. You always were someone. You didn't need Charlie to teach you that."

"I just wish he'd told me what to do when he was gone." The hitch was back in her voice. She climbed onto a stool, rested her head on her hands.

Gabe slid two coffee mugs across the counter and rounded the corner, a smug expression on his face.

Suspicious, she sniffed. "This isn't coffee."

"Nope. It's orange spice something or other." He gingerly sat on the stool next to her, balancing a real cup of coffee.

"Why?"

"You don't like coffee, and you should drink what you like." The smug look reappeared.

"How on earth did you figure that? I've worked in the coffee shop for seven years and nobody ever suspected." Sailor's heartbeat ratcheted up, the pounding having nothing to do with the caffeine in her cup.

Gabe leaned his head on his hand and closed his eyes. "I'm observant. You always pour yourself a cup and carry it around. You enjoy the aroma and the feel of it in your hands, but you never, ever drink it."

"Humph."

He cracked one speculative golden-brown eye. "What does 'humph' mean?"

"It means you're not supposed to notice stuff like that."

"Why, am I getting too close?" He pushed her with his elbow.

She didn't answer, couldn't. In the space of a few days, he'd discovered things about her that people who had known her for years didn't know, simply by being observant. By just…being Gabe.

In that short span of time, he'd managed to get under defenses that had taken her years to build. And she'd gone and done the unthinkable. She'd been depending on him. What would she do when he was gone? Would she be able to repair her life when he strode out of it? Because he would—whether he meant to or not.

"It's not that difficult a question. You don't have to think that hard, honey."

"Yes." She nearly whispered it, couldn't meet his eyes. "You're getting too close."

The back door slammed open. Chloe appeared, coughing, in a cloud of black smoke. She slammed the laptop on the countertop. "Your house is on fire."

EIGHT

Smoke still drifted from the wreckage of Sailor's carriage house, wisping gray into the pink evening sky. The fire inspector was inside, with Maria dogging his every step. Gabe crossed his arms. Another deliberate attempt to hurt Sailor. Maybe not meant to harm her physically, but emotionally, definitely.

Or the fire could possibly have been set to hide some evidence that the killer thought she might have? The books, maybe. The street rat, Chloe, had been in there just before the fire started. She could easily have set it and then reported it.

Footsteps crunched behind him. Jake Rollins, the pastor of Sailor's church, walked up. The former firefighter was dressed in full gear, his protective coat now unbuttoned and his helmet under his arm. He rolled out for fires to be with the victims, and to be there for the firefighters who risked so much on the job.

He stopped at Gabe's side, planted his feet in a wide stance. "Any word?"

"Not yet. You spoke to Sailor?" Part of the pastor's job as the fire department chaplain included spending time with victims.

"She's tough, but the loss of her home is a blow."

"Why is it that sometimes God feels the farthest away when we need Him the most?" Gabe glanced from the blackened shell of a house to Jake, who took the question in stride.

"Sometimes circumstances make God seem distant. Sometimes we're the ones pushing Him away. But if you believe God loves you, and He does, you have to cling to what you know—God may be unseen, but He'll never leave you."

"Have you always been this annoyingly right?"

Jake laughed, but his eyes held shadows. "No. Wilderness times happen to everyone. Even preachers. Maybe even especially preachers."

Sailor came out the back door with a white bakery bag and a to-go cup. "Here's something for the road, Jake."

"You're too good to me, Sailor." He slung his free arm around her neck. "That wouldn't be fresh-baked scones in there, would it?"

Gabe tamped down a rising sense of jealousy at their easy camaraderie. He didn't suspect the pastor of anything but trying to be a friend, but then again, why wouldn't the guy want to be more than friends with Sailor?

Gabe scowled. "So, you getting out of here, Jake?"

With a faintly surprised look, Jake smiled, then turned to Sailor. "Call me if you need anything. You have my numbers."

"Jake." Gabe nodded at the former firefighter, good guy, pastor, who'd been around to be Sailor's friend when he couldn't.

"Yeah, see you around, Gabe."

Maria stalked out the front door, smoke swirling around her in a foggy cloud. She pulled a mask off her face and shook soot out of her streaky curls.

"What's the word?"

"Traces of accelerant. It looks like the fires were set in two places. We've got pieces of what look like detonators. I think the fires started when Chloe opened the door. A modern building might not have gone up so quickly. I'm sorry, Sailor."

"Did you find any evidence that someone had broken in? Or that someone else had been there?" Gabe asked.

"We found this." Maria pulled an evidence bag out of her pocket. "Is the coin yours?"

Sailor took the bag and studied the coin, about the size of a quarter. "I've never seen it before. It looks like an award or something."

Maria stuffed the evidence bag back in her pocket. "It could be the break we're looking for. I'm taking it to the lab to see if we can identify it. If we're extremely lucky, we'll get enough of a print off it to match."

"Keep us posted." Gabe placed a hand at Sailor's back as they walked back to the coffee shop.

As they walked in the door, Layla stepped to the hall door and held out her arms. Sailor flew into them, pushing both of them into the room with the coffee bar.

"Layla. Are you all right?" She stepped back far enough to look into her eyes. "You're exhausted."

"I'm fine, sweetie, just a little worn around the edges. I had to come check on you. It's what Charlie would have wanted."

Sailor's new girl, Chloe, stepped around Layla and pushed a cup of coffee into Sailor's hands. "It's not as good as your nonfat, sugar-free vanilla latte, but it'll do in a pinch."

Sailor cupped the mug, holding it close.

"What happened? Does anyone know?" Layla tucked a wayward curl behind her ear.

Gabe pushed the back door closed. "It was definitely arson, though the inspector won't say that for sure until he gets the results back from his lab."

"Why now? I just don't get it. I'm not even staying here." Frustration eked out in her voice.

Gabe nipped the cup of coffee out of Sailor's hands, winking at her as he did. "Whoever did this wants you off your game, distressed and focused on what happened rather than the investigation."

"They searched the house before. Do you think there might have been something they didn't want me to find or keep?"

Layla put an arm around Sailor's back. "I'm going to duck out of here, doll. I need to get back to work."

"Thank you so much for being here, Layla. It means a lot to me—that you would come now."

Gabe poured the coffee down the sink, catching a glimpse of Layla leaving, Chloe right behind her. As much as he wanted to trust that the teenager was trying to turn her life around, he couldn't quite buy into it.

Sailor dropped into a café chair. "I should feel better back at work, in familiar surroundings. But I feel like a person whose safety net is being snipped one cord at a time and before long that net is just going to be one gigantic hole."

"That could have something to do with the fact that someone is making your life miserable." Maria, always tactful, shoved her hands in her jacket pocket. "I'm out of here."

As Maria slammed the kitchen door behind her, Sailor said, "Isn't there something I can do to draw them out? I'm getting a little tired of the victim gig."

Gabe stiffened. "We are not going to put you in harm's way. There are other ways to handle this than using you as bait. In fact, I think you should consider leaving town. As this escalates, there's no telling what they'll try to do."

"I'm trained, Gabe, not exactly a pushover. I've taken classes."

He knew that she could protect herself, but this situation was completely different. He pushed words out behind tightly clenched teeth. "Letting you be bait for a known subject with identifiable skills is one thing. Letting you play chicken with an unsub whose skill level is possibly higher than our own is downright stupid. I know you're anxious to catch the killers, but putting yourself in even more danger is not the way to do it."

"I know that. I'm just so sick of being a puppet on a string. I want to be in control of *something*." She stalked to the sink behind the counter, plunking mugs in.

"I'm sorry, Sailor. I know this situation stinks, but it will end. I promise."

In answer, she plopped a box of sweetener packets on the table and began refilling the containers.

Gabe pulled out his BlackBerry and started scrolling through e-mails. He had some news from the lab that the SBPD used for ballistics testing.

"What is it, Gabe?"

"The son, Ken." Gabe picked a stir stick up from the table, tapped it. "Apparently, the lab matched the ballistics from Charlie's murder to a murder in Ken's office about eight months ago. No one was caught. Ken was questioned, but he had an airtight alibi as he did for the night Charlie was murdered.

"The detectives who investigated think that it was a drug hit. There's been talk for years of a local connection to a high-powered dealer somewhere. That office building where Ken worked seemed to be at the epicenter. A lot of rich recreational users, easy access, lots of flow. The guy who was killed was what the other workers dubbed a 'goody-goody.' He was relatively new to the office and this area, less than a year. His wife said that he'd gotten very moody and depressed lately. The cops first guessed drugs, but his system tested clean, so he wasn't using. The detectives now think that he figured out the drug connection and was about to blow it for all of them."

Sailor spoke slowly as she reasoned it out. "So, you think that what's going on now could be somehow related to the drug ring that's running out of downtown?"

Gabe leaned his chair back to balance on two legs. "It fits. The money being laundered through here, the ballistics match. Sailor, didn't you tell me that you'd hired an independent auditor?"

Sailor's hands, busy refilling the packets of sugar and other sweeteners, stilled. Her wide eyes locked with Gabe's.

Gabe's chair legs hit the floor with a thump.

She *had*.

She had ordered an audit and by doing so had signed Charlie's death warrant.

Her face white and drawn, the cut on her forehead standing out in sharp relief, Sailor shuffled the same four packets of sugar over and over. "I did order an audit. I wanted to follow the money and find out which parts of the business made the most money for the coffee shop and capitalize on that."

"So Charlie knew you'd find out there was more money going through the accounts than Sip This was making. He must have told whoever that their gravy train through the coffee shop was about to come to an end."

"And that's what got him killed." She raised her eyes from the sugar packets—guilt evident in the green depths.

Gabe wanted to tell her she wasn't to blame, but telling her wouldn't mean anything. She needed to come to the conclusion on her own. "There's a ballistics connection between the guy in Kenneth's office and Charlie. Whoever killed Charlie must have known the audit would be stalled out until the will cleared probate, but they probably also assumed Kenny would inherit the controlling interest in the business."

He tapped the stir stick. "Kenny's up to his armpits in this, but he's not talking. There's no evidence he's involved. He's been questioned more than once, and your brother's on his way to pick him up again. But I don't think he's smart enough or has the connections to be the brains behind this organization. He's probably scared he's going to be the next corpse if he's not very, very careful."

Sailor rubbed her chest, where he knew the knot sat, the burden that came from the belief that she'd been responsible for the death of her mentor and friend. "So this isn't really about protecting nine thousand dollars a day."

Gabe slid his chair closer and wrapped his arm around her slim shoulders, shoulders trying to carry so much weight for so many. "No, honey. This is about protecting an empire. Sip This and Charlie became the weak link, but nine thousand dollars a day is probably a drop in the bucket."

"I thought it was my fault." Her eyes brimmed and she blinked.

She rubbed at her eyes with the palm of her hand, so impatient that he had to smile. "No way. What happened to Charlie was set in motion long before you called that auditor. Honey, we're lucky that they didn't decide to take you out instead because the end result with the audit would have been the same."

It could have been that Charlie was protecting her or it could have been that he was the convenient target that night. If she had been in the building that night, she most likely would've been the murder victim. A fact that made his toenails curl.

The floor creaked overhead. Gabe rose to his feet in one smooth motion. "Get in the bathroom and lock the door."

Her eyes were wide and terrified as he closed her in the tiny room. He waited for the lock to slide home before he silently took the stairs. A crack of light beamed out from Sailor's office.

Gripping his weapon in a stance as natural as breathing, he kicked the door open.

Sailor's special project, Chloe, had her hand stuck in a file drawer. Slowly, she raised both to shoulder level. "Sailor told me I could work on the files."

"Not those files. Try again."

An irritated look flashed in her eyes, but she squelched it. He walked closer.

"You wanna put that thing away? It could go off and someone might get hurt. Namely me."

"What are you doing here, Chloe? First the fire right after you were in Sailor's house, and now you're in the office going through stuff. What's the matter? Didn't find what you were looking for the first time?"

"I didn't set the fire. And I don't have to answer your questions."

Gabe tucked his gun back in the holster on his hip and advanced slowly. "You can talk to me here, or you can talk at the station in an interrogation room. And I can assure you that I'm much nicer than her brother will be."

"You have no cause to take me in."

He grabbed her wrist and, using his body for leverage, flipped her around, pressing her face flat against the wall. "Tell it to the judge."

She struggled against him, one futile lunge backward, before quieting as he tightened the nylon zip tie around her wrists. "I'm FBI, you jerk."

Of course she was. "Where's your ID?"

"Back pocket."

He pulled out a small folded wallet, the gold badge inside the cred case clearly identifying her. "Nice interdepartmental cooperation, Special Agent Davis."

She smirked but didn't rise to the bait. "This shop has

been under suspicion for laundering money, and I wasn't about to tell Lieutenant Conyers that we're heading up an investigation with his sister as the target."

"Sailor didn't know anything about the money."

"I know that...now. But someone around here did, or does." She held out her wrists, and with a hard look, he cut off the restraints with his knife.

"What have you found out?"

"Nothing that you haven't."

Gabe didn't believe her, but he also knew she wouldn't tell him anything. "I don't care what you're doing here, Davis. Investigate to your heart's content. My first priority—only priority—is keeping Sailor safe. You get in the way of that and I'll take you out."

She rubbed her wrists. "Agreed. So we'll keep this little conversation to ourselves?"

"Fine." He walked to the door, turned back. "What were you, in middle school when you were recruited?"

She looked up from the desk. "Like I haven't ever heard that one before."

Downstairs, he knocked on the bathroom door. "It's me. We're all clear."

Sailor's face was white and drawn as she opened the door. She was shaking.

"Hey, Sailor, it's not as bad as all that. It was just Chloe."

She turned her BlackBerry around to face him. A photo had loaded onto the color screen. A child swinging on a playground gym. Dressed in private-school plaid, her feet reached for the sky. Her head thrown back, she looked into the camera...with vivid green eyes.

He read the words beneath the picture, then read them again, trying to make sense of what he was seeing. *DID YOU REALLY THINK WE COULDN'T FIND HER?*

Sailor could feel the familiar square shape of her PDA, but it didn't feel like a cell phone. It felt like a weapon she wanted to throw across the room, shatter into a million pieces. She recognized the shock, but it was soul-deep fear that threatened to swallow her up, now that Gabe was here. It bore down like a big black tornado cloud barreling at her, eating everything in its path, wanting to whisk her up in its hungry, whirling winds.

Oxygen vanished as those black clouds narrowed her eyesight. She gasped for air, hitting the cold porcelain tile floor with her knees, grasping the sink for balance as the room reeled. Her PDA went skidding across the floor.

Arms closed around her. She almost thought to fight, but she didn't have the energy, not while her sole focus was getting air. Her chest hurt so bad.

She couldn't even think about her baby girl. Not…yet.

The strong arms holding her disappeared, and she sagged, knocking her head on the edge of the sink. Seconds later, Gabe pressed one of her bakery bags to her lips and pulled her onto into a chair in the kitchen. "Breathe into the bag, honey. That's right, nice and slow."

The hand supporting her began rubbing her back— large, looping circles—and slowly, as he rubbed, the constriction in her chest eased and she was able to take a breath.

She let her head fall back onto Gabe's shoulder. "You're—always—coming to my rescue." Her breath still wasn't quite all there, but the blind panic had receded.

Gabe let Sailor rest in his arms and let his heart rate return to normal. He needed to hold her right now, needed this moment of calm as much as she seemed to. "Sailor, you want to tell me what's going on?"

She hiccuped a breath. "We've got to find her."

He picked up the PDA. The little girl looked to be about seven years old. "She's yours?"

At his look, she crumpled. "I think so, I don't know. I haven't seen her since she was just hours old."

"Do you have any idea where she is?"

"I have a letter and a picture the adoptive mother sent when she was about three months old. I went through an adoption agency and they handled the contact."

"I want to see the letter and I need the name of the agency you went through. If they have computer files, Maria can access them." He paced the room, coming to a stop in front of her. On his face and in his warm brown eyes, she saw equal parts of compassion and determination. "We'll find her, don't worry."

Missing a daughter she'd never known had been such an ever-present ache that she wouldn't know what to do if it wasn't there. Except now Sailor had this huge, incredibly pressing sense of urgency to get to her, to wrap the little girl in her arms and keep her safe.

Reminding herself that it wasn't her right didn't seem to do much good, but she had to remember it. All she could do was warn her baby's real parents to be vigilant and so, so watchful for their little girl's safety.

So many times when she'd wanted to depend on other people, she'd been let down. Her older brother, rightfully, had left home to join the police force. But in doing so, he'd left her alone. Her mother had always chosen her next fix over taking care of dependent children. She thought Charlie had been the exception, but she was wrong.

She'd made herself independent. But she couldn't do this on her own—she needed Gabe. As much as she hated to ask for help, she had to. "Please, Gabe, help me find my baby."

NINE

Gabe watched Sailor make it into Cruse's house where Bayley would set the high-tech alarm system. Patrol units were scheduled to drive by at twenty-minute intervals. They were safe.

At least physically. Sailor had a tiny T-shirt clutched in her fist as she went in, one her baby girl had worn in the hospital. Sailor was still standing and walking, smiling, even after all the hits she'd taken. She didn't realize herself how strong she'd become.

She seemed content to lean on him now. Only someone with no sense at all would fail to recognize she needed protection in these circumstances. But what would Sailor do once she didn't need him anymore? Would she stick around or would she leave him dangling again?

From his parents to Sailor to his superior officers, he'd spent his whole life longing to be chosen, whispering in his heart, *pick me. Pick me over your work. Pick me over your fears. Pick me to be the best.*

A car behind him on the beach road honked impatiently. He drove forward with a roar, leaving the memories behind in a cloud of dust.

Over the years, he'd let go of that child looking for affirmation. From the beginning of time God had picked him to be His adopted son and that was the one choice that mattered. The others he had to leave up to God. And now he had to give this relationship to God, too, no matter how scary it was.

He looked down at the worn photo of a baby girl. Right now Sailor needed him to find her child. And he would do anything in his power to do that, to keep the long fingers of this unknown attacker from reaching Sailor's little girl.

Maria could help.

He strode into the lab, the glass door whooshing shut behind him. "Maria, I need you to trace this photo. I've got a letter that might help narrow it down regionally."

"Hang on, cowboy. Hand me the photo." Maria slid across the floor in her rolling chair, passing Gabe a sheet of paper as she took the photo.

"What's this?" He studied the sheet, a photo of a fingerprint clipped to the top.

"Your ticket to interview Kenneth Williams Banks. It's his fingerprint on the coin found in Sailor's cottage."

A slow smile spread across Gabe's face. "You are a gifted one, Ms. Fuentes."

"Naturally." She studied the back of the photograph. "Looks like we have a photographer's mark made in the printing. I may be able to track it down for you. Let me see the letter."

He handed it to her, peering over her shoulder as she studied the postmark.

"It came through Pensacola, but that doesn't mean it was mailed there. Can you leave this with me?" Maria brushed her curls back over her shoulder with an impatient push.

"Do you think you can find her?"

"Mmm." She didn't lift her gaze from the postmark. "I need the hospital where she was born, the agency Sailor went through for the adoption, and any other details Sailor remembers."

Gabe pulled a piece of paper from his pocket. "This is everything."

Maria took the paper from him. "Okay, slick. Let me see where I can get with this while you interview the coffee baron."

"I need the coin."

She handed it to him in an evidence bag. "Sign the log. We need to keep chain of custody intact."

"Don't worry. I'm going to find out what he knows. And if he's behind this madness, I'm going to nail him to the wall."

"That's a lot to do in one night. You better get going." She whizzed back across the floor as the doors slid shut behind him. Not patient enough to wait for the elevator, Gabe took the stairs up two at a time. He looked at the coin in his hand. It might just be the key to breaking Ken Banks's silence.

The next morning, Sailor sat on the porch swing at Cruse's, gently rocking it with her foot. The cup of tea Bayley made her rapidly cooled in her hand, Scruffydog on guard at her feet. Her fear for her child was nearly palpable at times. Overlying it was a low evil certainty that she knew the killer and she knew him well. That person knew her well enough to know that she'd had a child—a girl, and that child had been adopted seven years ago.

She looked at the bright blue depthless sky. "Are you taking care of her, God? Please, Father, stand guard over her."

Her sister-in-law shoved open the sliding glass door, long brown curls flying in the breeze, and settled in the swing beside Sailor. She tossed a fleece blanket over the two of them. "So what's going on between you and Gabe?"

Despite her fear, Sailor managed a laugh. "Get straight to the point, don't you?"

"You don't have time for long conversations when someone is trying to kill you. Believe me, I know."

Sailor bit her bottom lip. "I wish I could say nothing, but that wouldn't be true."

"I think it would be awesome."

Bayley had overcome huge obstacles in her relationship with Cruse. Not only her own fears, but Cruse's reticence to share their family's not-so-perfect past with her. But just because Bayley and Cruse had been able to get through their respective issues and come through on the other side, that didn't mean it was possible for everyone—even though the glowing newlywed obviously wanted to spread her happiness around.

Sailor sipped her tea. "There's a lot of history between me and Gabe. I'm just not sure we can forget about the past long enough to build a future together."

"Do you love him?"

Bayley's characteristic bluntness made Sailor smile again. "It doesn't matter if I do."

Bayley shot her a look, her dark blue eyes full of

reproach. "Of course it matters. He spent the night here last night after you went to bed. Cruse tried to tell him you were fine, but he wouldn't leave. In fact, he insisted on staying to make sure you were safe through the night."

Sailor pushed out of the swing, her legs suddenly restless. Walking to the edge of the porch, she looked toward the waves, somersaulting, twisting, rolling in their bid to reach shore. Running back when they came too far in to the sand. She felt that way—tumbled and tossed, and when she stepped too close, she had to run back to the safety of the life she knew.

"It's just not that simple, Bayley. Even when all this is over—if it ever is—I'm not sure we can forget about the past."

"I didn't think I was ready for a relationship, and I was right. I'd never been allowed to find out who I was. I couldn't reach out to Cruse until I knew I was a whole person, and then I was ready to be a couple."

"Are you saying you don't think I'm a whole person?"

Bayley brought the blanket and wrapped it around Sailor's shoulders. "No, but I am saying I think you've been protected—and protected yourself—long enough. It's time to think about what you really want from your life and go after it. Don't just stick with what you know because it's the path of least resistance. I see it all the time in the shelter. Women don't leave a life that makes them miserable because they can't see the future holds something so much better."

"I don't know what the future holds."

Bayley laughed, and Sailor could hear the full-bellied abandonment that had made her so irresistible to Cruse. "That's what makes life so interesting. Come on."

"Where?"

"Trust me." Bayley led Sailor into the house, stopping outside the door to the storage closet in the hall. "Cruse would probably kill me if he knew I was showing you this. But it's time, Sailor. Take the step. I'll be in my room if you need me."

She threw open the door to the closet and walked away, the dog padding behind her.

Sailor stood at the closet door. Inside was an easel, a dozen canvases, a box of paints and a cup full of brushes. With trembling fingers, she reached for a brush, nearly stopping herself, but she touched it, running her fingers across the soft bristles. Cruse had bought every kind, round and filbert, bright and flat, synthetic for her acrylics and sable for times when she felt like using watercolors.

She hadn't painted since the attack when she was seventeen. She'd tried a couple of times, but it had felt like a falsehood, something learned in childhood that was no longer applicable. Had she just been afraid? That her feelings, so deep and volatile, would be too overwhelming? That even her art couldn't put a Band-Aid on the wound left behind?

She was so tired of being scared. Grabbing the easel and the first canvas on the stack, she went back to the porch. The paints and brushes were next, and a Mason jar full of water. No time for oils to dry; she would use versatile acrylic.

It didn't hurt to squeeze the paint onto her palette.

Dipping the brush in the vibrant green didn't cause a nuclear meltdown. But touching the paint to the canvas—she wasn't sure she could make the first stroke.

Taking a huge gulp of the moist salty air, she dabbed a little of the sea-green onto the canvas. The stab of pain in the heart region didn't hurt too badly. In fact, it felt kinda good. She was taking a deliberate step away from past hurts and reclaiming her future for herself. More sea-colored paints went onto the canvas: aqua, white, gray, and bright bluebird for the crisp, late-autumn sky.

Bit by bit, the ocean appeared. And bit by bit, the hurt and pain leached out of her. Worry for her daughter still lingered, but she poured it onto the canvas. And knowing she and Gabe were doing everything they could to find her daughter, Sailor could simply paint.

Gabe knocked on Ken Banks's door. When the door cracked open, he pushed into the stockbroker's house. Banks's eyes rounded, his pupils shrinking to a pinpoint. "Wha-what's going on?"

"You tell me, *Kenneth*." Gabe dangled the evidence bag holding the coin in front of his face. "Ever seen this before?"

Banks swallowed, his Adam's apple moving convulsively.

"Think carefully before you lie."

Ken Banks ran a hand through straight sandy-blond hair. "Okay, I have one like that. But it's an award I won at work—it's attached to a plaque by my desk."

"Have you ever carried it around in your pocket?"

"Maybe, yeah. When I first got the award, I kind of rubbed it in to some of the guys at work."

As Ken trailed off, Gabe let silence stretch between them, just in case Charlie's son had something to add. When Ken didn't move, Gabe eased back but didn't let down his guard. "Show me the plaque."

Ken blinked. "Yeah, sure. This way."

Gabe followed Ken into the waterfront condo. It had rich wood floors, but very little furniture. A few nails and faded squares on the wall indicated he'd once had artwork, but no longer. "You moving, Ken?"

"No. Why would you…oh. I've had some cash-flow problems lately." He laughed, a nervous high-pitched whinny.

In the office, a back room that overlooked a court-yard, Ken waved his hand at the bookshelves. "I won the award last year for the most trades one quarter. I can't remember which."

Gabe looked at the plaques lining the shelves. "Which one matches this coin?"

Ken pointed to the bottom shelf. "It's uh, that one."

Gabe angled his body so he could see the plaque and still keep Banks in his line of vision. "There's no coin there."

Banks dropped to his knees to look on the shelf, moving the plaques to look behind them. "Someone must have taken it."

"Right, because that's really logical."

Ken sat back on his heels. "No, Sloan, I swear, I didn't know it was missing until just now. I haven't carried that thing around in months." He paused. "Listen, do you want a cup of coffee or something? I've got some beans that were roasted over at the coffee shop."

"Sure, whatever." Gabe didn't want anything this guy brewed. What he wanted was to know what Ken Banks was hiding.

While Banks started the coffee, Gabe looked around the condo. Did the down-on-his-luck stockbroker need money badly enough to kill for it? "There was a murder in your office less than a year ago."

The coffee grinder hiccupped and then resumed grinding.

Gabe walked farther into the kitchen. "Most people go their whole lives without knowing someone who was murdered. And here you are, Ken. Two people that you knew, possibly even two people you were close to, were killed. Makes me think I wouldn't want to be your friend."

Ken poured water into the pot and turned it on. "I was never accused of that crime. I had an alibi. Just like I have an alibi for the night my father was killed."

"Yeah, just like." Gabe fingered the coin inside the plastic evidence bag, looked at it thoughtfully. "So how did a coin that only has your fingerprint on it get to Sailor's house if you didn't drop it there?"

"I don't know, man. Maybe somebody stole it."

"Who else has been in your apartment?"

"My dad. Layla. Some guys from the office for poker night. I don't know who could have taken it. Maybe I left the door unlocked."

"Yeah, Ken, it makes a lot of sense that someone would break in your apartment and steal an award that has no meaning to anyone but you."

When Ken's right eye twitched, Gabe went in for the kill. "Where were you yesterday when Sailor's house was set on fire?"

Ken turned away, poured a cup of coffee into a black ceramic mug. When his hands shook, he laid them palms flat on the glassy countertop.

"Where were you, Ken?"

"At work."

Gabe spoke two languages and bits of an obscure African dialect. And he could tell a liar in any language because discerning a lie didn't have anything to do with the words the person said. It was all about body language and behavior. And Ken Banks had just told a whopper. Was he stupid enough to think Gabe wouldn't check?

"I'm going to ask if anyone saw you at the office, Ken."

The stockbroker closed his eyes. "I wasn't at work. I quit two weeks ago."

"*Before* your father died?"

"The pressure there…you just wouldn't believe." He stirred cream into his coffee, but didn't drink, just laid the spoon down and stared at it.

"Where were you yesterday?"

"I was at a meeting. Narcotics Anonymous. You can ask my sponsor. He was there, too. We had lunch together after."

"Write his name and number down."

After Ken scribbled the information on a paper towel, Gabe tucked it into his pocket and walked into the front room. "What are you doing for money, Ken? How do you expect to live?"

"I'll find another job. I needed some time to get on my feet."

"And right now?"

"You might have noticed I don't have a lot of stuff. Those are not decorating choices I'm making. I'm selling my stuff so I can eat. I'm trying to sell the condo, but the market's not so great right now."

He opened the door and Gabe stepped out on the stoop. "Am I a suspect?"

"I'd call you a person of interest." While Ken was still processing that one, Gabe pointed to the empty spot over the fireplace where four unadorned hooks were attached to the wall. "What happened to your guns?"

"Sold them. I never hunted or anything, but they were my grandfather's, or so I was told."

"Who did you sell them to?"

"A dealer down on W Street. I've probably got a receipt somewhere."

"You find it, give me a call. See you around, Ken."

Gabe took the sidewalk to his truck. He slid into the truck, cranked the engine and as he drove away, he saw Ken Banks on the front porch of his waterfront condo, staring at the grass.

That was one mixed-up guy trying to put his life together. Or the other option: a smart killer hiding his trail.

Hours later, Sailor heard the knock on the door, and heard Bayley talking, but it wasn't until she felt Gabe standing behind her that she stopped painting and turned around. His eyes were suspiciously shiny. "What?"

He chuckled, wrapped his arms around her and lifted her off the ground, swinging her in a circle.

"Gabe, stop. You're getting paint on your shirt."

He set her on her feet, but didn't let go, sliding his right hand down her arm to hold on to her fingers. He looked down. "Well, so I did. Now we match."

When she looked at her black silk T-shirt, part of her extensive Sip This wardrobe, she realized she was covered in smudges and blobs of multicolored paint. "I was really tired of black, anyway. I think we look just about perfect."

She stepped back, narrowed her eyes, considered. "Except there's something missing…right there." She dabbed blue-green paint on the end of Gabe's nose.

He lunged for the paintbrush and she squealed, turning to run for the door. Locked. She wheeled around, brandishing the brush. "Not another step."

Gabe stepped closer.

"I mean it. I have a weapon and I'm not afraid to use it."

His brown eyes lit, glimmering gold in the bright afternoon light. He brushed a hand through her hair, his touch so gentle her throat threatened to close. "What are you doing?"

"Just looking at you. You're beautiful."

"Gabe."

"Shh."

He reached for her waist and pulled her closer. His lips grazed hers, a butterfly touch. She closed her eyes.

His hand dove into her hair, shredding her ponytail and leaving it streaming down her back as he drew her closer. She should push him away. She didn't want this, couldn't trust the feelings coursing through her. Depending on him would hurt too much. How could she make him understand?

She couldn't. Because he was a protector, always had been as long as she'd known him. From the first time she'd met him—she stood up for the kittens, he stood up for her. He'd been standing up for her all the years in between, too. She just hadn't realized it. Her arm crept around his neck and she held on.

Here was warmth and security, and even though she felt like Dorothy in the middle of the tornado, it wasn't fear she felt, just the thrill of holding him in her arms.

His phone beeped. Without letting go of her, his eyes locked with hers, he reached to his belt and thumbed the button. He glanced at the message and she saw the transformation. In an instant, he hardened into a cop, with a cop's dark, unreadable expression.

"What is it?"

"We have to go. Maria found your daughter."

Eden, Florida, turned out to be a picturesque southern town at the Alabama state line. Wide porches loaded with mums and pumpkins, hay bales and the occasional scarecrow gave nod to the harvest season in this still-agricultural area.

Sailor noted every detail, memorized each shop front and street corner in her daughter's hometown. "Are you sure this is it? Are you sure she's the one?"

Patiently Gabe answered again, for the tenth—twelfth?—time. "Yes, Sailor. I'm as sure as I can be."

"How did Maria find her?"

"A bribe here, a break-in there. The usual." Gabe smiled.

"Don't joke about this. She found her by computer records, right?"

Cruising through the town as if they were just out for a morning drive, Gabe rolled the windows down, and a cool November breeze whisked the stale air out of the car, bringing with it the scent of boiled peanuts and freshly turned earth. "I love this time of year."

"Gabe…"

"Maria followed the computer trail from the hospital, but when she got to the Department of Children and Families, she needed local records before she could get into the court system files to find a name and address. She got them and here we are."

She wouldn't ask again. Because he was right. Here they were. In her daughter's town. If Sailor closed her eyes, she could imagine a towheaded toddler coming out of the drugstore with a fat lollipop or a sturdy five-year-old batting off the tee in the ballpark across the street with her dad coaching her to first base. For the first time, she let herself think about what her daughter looked like skipping out of the church in her Sunday best, holding her mom's and dad's hands.

These things had always been too painful to dwell on before. But now, the pain reminded Sailor that life was precious and sometimes painful. The ache had always been there. Despite her best efforts to keep it away, she'd always wondered, always prayed her daughter was happy and secure and loved in her family.

And a secret part of her hoped her child's parents told her that her birth mother loved her, too. Because she did. Oh, how she did. From the first moment she'd seen that squalling red newborn with her mouth wide open to breathe in the world, she'd known she would never be the same again. That somewhere on this planet, her heart would be walking around outside her body, and she wouldn't be able stand it if anything happened to her baby.

"How do you want to handle this?" Gabe spoke quietly, as if he knew her thoughts were too full, that if he jarred her, some random emotion might come spilling out.

She'd prayed about it and thought it through from all different angles the whole two-hour drive to this small southern town. It was the right thing to do. "I think you need to talk to them. If I go to the door, if I appear this unexpectedly, the parents are going to be frightened. Not for her safety, but for fear I'll try to take her away. We've already figured out they're good people if they turn out to be like they look on paper. So you talk to them, okay?"

"If that's the way you want to handle it, that's what we'll do." Gabe's hand, warm and reassuring, closed over her chilly fingers. So much could go wrong.

Gabe turned into a driveway just down the block and across the street from the local elementary school. The house itself was a warm redbrick Georgian, the kind of house that Sailor drew as a child, when the teachers asked her to draw a picture of her house. Inviting and friendly, ivy growing up the face, the house looked loved. How could the child not be?

He parked and took a long last look at Sailor. "You should be perfectly safe here in the car, but if you see something out of the ordinary, or if you get scared, call my cell phone or come in the house. Don't wait."

"I promise."

Gabe strode to the door. He'd changed clothes, wearing a suit and his SBPD badge to put the parents at ease.

The front door opened and a slender brunette peered out. Her jeans gave her a casual, friendly air, but a slim corduroy jacket made the outfit seem stylish. Gabe showed her his identification, spoke earnestly. She crossed her arms, looked at the car. Finally, almost reluctantly, she opened the door far enough for Gabe to enter the house.

He sent a wink at Sailor before easing inside. The door closed behind him.

She forced herself to take a deep breath. It would be fine. It would have to be fine.

Smoothing her cotton skirt, she stared alternately at the clock and the front door of the house, lifting a silent prayer as her nerves seemed to rattle around inside her. He'd been in there ten minutes. How long could it take for Gabe to explain the dangerous situation?

A black Lexus screeched to the curb in front of the house. Sailor's thumb hovered over the speed dial to Gabe's cell phone, but as she began to press the button, she saw a child fling open the back door of the car. The girl, maybe her daughter, hopped out onto the curb and pulled a backpack, nearly her own size, thumping to the ground behind her.

Sailor leaned forward to watch the little girl, petite and wiry, pretty blond hair pulled into a high ponytail. Her heart recognized that the child not forty feet away from her was the child she had borne—the daughter she'd given away to a better life.

The ache in her chest intensified as she watched the scene in the yard unfold like a movie.

The woman—the mother—opened the front door. A chocolate-brown Labrador retriever nosed around her, caught sight of the little girl and rocketed across the yard to yelp and flip-flop in circles as the sweetheart dragged her backpack across the leaf-strewn yard toward the house.

The dad—at least Sailor guessed it was the dad—came behind to meet the mother and child in the middle of the front yard. The mom bent to her daughter and sent her into the house.

A quick protest that Sailor could imagine. "Oh, Mom, I want to stay out here with Roscoe." But Mom held her ground, and the little girl dragged her way into the house.

Then the father questioned. The mother nodded, and answered, probably sharing what Gabe had explained to her. Both of them, simultaneously, looked at the car where Sailor sat, feeling suddenly exposed like an oyster on a cracker, ready for the chomping.

The father followed the little girl into the house, shooing the dog in front of him, shook hands with Gabe at the door. The mother stood still in the yard, staring across the street into the tree line, perhaps looking for danger, hoping she wouldn't find it.

Then the woman headed straight for the car where Sailor sat. She opened the door and slid into the driver's seat. Sailor blinked. What did she say—oh dear God, what did she say to the woman who raised her baby?

"I'm Alicia." Her soft brown eyes, glowing with a mother's determination and a hint of tears, met Sailor's. "I had to speak to you—to say thank you."

"For what?" Sailor whispered, her throat clogged with her own tears.

"For my daughter, for having her best interests always, always in your heart." Alicia paused and reached for Sailor's hand. "I know I'm her mother. But you are, too—a real mother who cares about what's best for her child. I can't thank you enough for what you've done for her, and for us."

How could she have known how desperately Sailor needed to hear those exact words? Alicia looked at their clasped hands, hesitated. When she looked up, the tears she'd been fighting spilled out. "Her name is Emily."

Sailor refused to wipe the evidence of emotion from her own face. *Emily*. "What a beautiful name."

Her eyes met Alicia's. They laughed, a slightly edgy release.

"She's a beautiful child. And she's happy. Well, except for when it's her turn to do the dishes."

"Alicia, you need to know I won't come here again. I had to be here today, but she's your child. I won't interfere with that, I promise." Sailor said the words. And she even meant them, but the knife of pain in her chest felt like she was being opened up without anesthesia.

Emily's mother squeezed her hand. "You're a good woman, Sailor Conyers. I'm so glad I met you."

Sailor closed her eyes. When she opened them again, Alicia was gone, but pressed in her hand, she found a photograph of Emily. Blond ponytail under a bright red ball cap, Emily looked strong and confident as she faced the camera.

Best of all, she wasn't the child Sailor had seen in the e-mail. Her child was safe, and thanks to Gabe and Maria, she would remain safe until the killers were caught.

Gabe slid into the car. "You okay?"

Sailor blinked, clearing the tears from her eyes for

the last time. "Yeah, I think so. You know the e-mailed photo wasn't Emily?"

"Yeah, I figured that out pretty much the second I walked in the house. Her parents probably have two hundred pictures of that kid in there. They handled it as well as could be expected, I think. They already have a good security system and they're all right with sticking close to home for a while. The police in this small town are friends of theirs. They're nice people, Sailor, and they love that kid. That much was obvious."

How could someone be happy and sad at the same time? God had blessed her with a beautiful daughter and had given her a way to make sure her daughter never had to suffer the kind of childhood Sailor had.

Seeing Emily and her parents answered a question Sailor had lived with for years. But seeing her, being that close and not being able to hold her, was its own special kind of torture.

A dark thought crossed her mind. "You don't think we led them to Emily, do you?"

"No. We were very, very careful."

"What about the other little girl? Do you think she's in danger?"

"I think that child was chosen only because of her similarity in coloring to you."

That these people—whoever they were—would go to such lengths to frighten her made her feel sick, a knot of worry and fear churning in her stomach. "They're really serious, the people who are out to scare me."

"Yes." Gabe pulled to a stop and looked into her eyes. "And they're not going to stop now."

TEN

Sailor looked up the stairs to the dark upper floor where she had her Sip This office. She hadn't been there since the night Charlie died—was murdered. It had been easy to avoid with all that had happened. But she had to face it some time. Now was the time. She needed clothes since hers burned in her carriage house. Luckily, because her cottage was so small, she had several rubber tubs of winter clothes in the storeroom at the coffee shop.

At the top of the stairs, the wide hall yawned, the rooms dark at this hour with no lights on. Silly to be afraid when she'd been here so many nights, but the events of the past few days had taught her caution, if nothing else.

Backing up a step, she bumped into someone. "Oh!"

"Can we talk?" Ken Banks crowded her on the stairs.

"How did you get in here?"

He held up a single key, dangling on the keychain. "I came in the back. I just want to talk, Sailor."

"I don't think that's a good idea." She glanced down the hall, no sign of Gabe.

"I don't want to argue, Sailor. I want to apologize."

Sailor glanced up again. Her office was the first one on the right. She forced herself to take the final three steps slowly and flipped the light switch on. "Have a seat."

Ken sat gingerly on the love seat while Sailor chose to sit in her desk chair, with the desk between them. She'd never trusted him. After finding his coin in her house after the fire, she had even less reason to do so, but she knew Gabe had to be close. His overprotective streak wouldn't let Ken get within ten feet of her without him being nearby. "What did you want to talk about?"

"I was angry when I found out you had the controlling interest in the coffee shop, but it wasn't because I thought I deserved it more than you. Really, it's the opposite. I knew I didn't deserve it."

He stopped and cleared his throat. "My dad was right to leave it to you. He knew you'd take care of the business and he probably thought I'd run it into the ground."

She tilted her head, considered. Was he telling the truth, or was this some new angle he'd figured he could work? "Okay, so…"

"Plain and simple, I was jealous of you. The relationship you had with my dad, the business—it was all effortless for you."

That was hardly the truth, but she could see how Ken would think that. "Why are you telling me this?"

"I want a second chance. I know you don't like me, and you have good reason." He scrubbed a hand over his thin face. "I've had a drug addiction. But I want— I'm ready to turn my life around."

"And you think you can do that here?"

"I need a way to support myself and I need to get away from my office. I've joined Narcotics Anonymous. I've been clean for four weeks and three days. I know it doesn't sound like much, but for an addict it's an eternity. Every day I get better."

His expression was a mixture of impossible hope and the expectation of sure rejection. How many times had she seen that exact face on her mother? And how many times had she been disappointed?

Why did Charlie leave her Sip This? Did he leave it to her because he knew she'd follow through on the auditor and Ken wouldn't? Because he knew she'd be strong?

"You want to work here."

It was a statement and he didn't refute it. "I'm one of the owners, Sailor. Even if you wanted to, you couldn't change that."

"You think the employees will accept you?"

"They already think I'm the new boss." He gave an apologetic shrug.

Sailor slowly nodded. He was *a* new boss. And as much as she'd loved working at Sip This, it was running the business that she enjoyed most. She didn't even like coffee, for goodness' sake. This place wasn't her calling. It had only taken Charlie getting killed, assassins chasing her, and her house getting burned down to figure it out.

Kenny was right; he didn't deserve a second chance. None of them did if it came right down to it. But Sailor believed in a God who specialized in second chances. In forgiveness instead of fear.

Could Kenny do it? She had no idea.

Did she have the guts to take control of her life? It was a huge step, but she had to be able to step out on her own. And if she'd learned anything from being forcibly ejected from her comfort zone, it was that. She wanted a real life, not a comfortable life.

So if Ken wanted to give this business a shot, he could have it. It was his birthright. She'd be around to give him a hand, but she wouldn't be here to be his babysitter. "Ken, I believe in second chances. Your father believed in them, too. But that means that every day, you have to face down hard decisions and make the right ones. You can start by treating my employees right."

"What? You mean you're going to let me run Sip This?" His incredulous face only convinced her she'd made the best decision, at least for now. Sometimes people needed to know you believed in them in order for them to make the hard choices.

"I'll maintain my fifty-one percent for one year. And at the end of the year, if we're making a profit and you're still clean, I'll sell my shares to you." Charlie had believed in her. He'd given her a chance. Now she was giving that chance to Charlie's son. She reached in her desk drawer for a card. "Here's the number of my pastor. He can help you find what you're looking for."

Ken Banks shot to his feet, taking the card from her hand. "I promise I won't disappoint you, Sailor." He barreled out of the room and down the stairs. She felt a momentary twinge of sadness, but it wasn't like she wouldn't be watching out for the place, making sure he did the job right.

Sailor pushed out of her chair and looked around the room Charlie had given to her as an office six years ago. It had her personality and her stamp. From the sand-colored walls to the light aqua-blue on the ceiling, it was her room.

Oddly, she didn't think she'd miss it that much. Picking a tote bag from her collection on the back of the door, she gathered the few things she wanted to keep from her office. The little figurine of the Space Needle she'd bought when she and Charlie had gone on a Seattle research trip, and a couple of recipe books she didn't want to replace. Her fingers lingered over a photograph.

Charlie had taken her out on the *Good Hope* for her first fishing trip. She hadn't wanted to fish, just sunbathe, but when she'd seen him reel in his first amberjack, she'd been captivated. He wanted her to try, but for an abused child who'd been told she was worthless her whole life, trying something that was so out of her comfort zone just seemed so…huge.

Finally, he'd talked her into it and she'd reeled in the biggest fish of the day. He had one of the boat's crew snap this photo of the two of them with her fish. She picked up the frame.

Strange, she'd never noticed that he'd written on the back. *Sailor, set your mind on your dreams, and you can do whatever you want.*

Tears welled again. She didn't know why he'd chosen the path he had. If Ken had been involved in drugs, perhaps Charlie was protecting his son by laundering the money. Maybe she would never know.

But once again, her mentor was giving her a nudge,

and God could give her the strength to follow *her* dream. Coffee had never been her passion, but the folk art she collected had. Maybe she could even open a little gallery down the street. She felt free for the first time in years. Free to make her own decisions, to follow *her* path.

Hurrying now, she raced into the hall, coming to a hasty halt when she caught sight of Gabe lounging against the wall opposite her office. "How long have you been there?"

He smiled—a lopsided, affectionate grin that made her heart turn over in one long, lazy loop. "Long enough. You sure you want him around here?"

"No. But it's the right thing to do. He owns half the business and I need some space to figure out what I want."

Gabe skimmed a finger down the side of her face. "Is it hard for you, giving up that control?"

"To him? Yes. I don't trust him."

"Me, either. And to tell you the truth, I'm not sure he'll ever have the chance to prove he means what he says. From what I hear, he's probably going to face drug charges at the very least in connection with the ring at his office. You ready to get out of here?"

"Just a sec. I want to grab some clothes out of the storeroom."

The upstairs bedrooms had long ago been converted to storage space. Sailor opened the door to the storeroom expecting to see neat stacks of clear Rubbermaid containers, but instead she found haphazard piles of cardboard boxes by the door. "What in the—"

"What is it?"

"These aren't supposed to be here." She took a look at the tracking labels. "They're from Island Accessories, one of Layla's companies under Sand Dollar Souvenirs. We order from them, but it looks like they were delivered to the wrong place."

She pulled open the box and lifted out two short pillar candles and one larger one with seashells set in the base. "I sell these downstairs and I can never keep them in stock. I wish Layla had meant to send these boxes here. I'm going to snag these three candles. She won't mind, and I'll reimburse her for the cost later."

Gabe cleared his throat. "Not to interrupt shopping or anything, but winter clothes?"

Sailor laughed, the freedom she'd started to feel when she painted singing through her system. She felt like she'd been given control over her life. Maybe she'd always had the power, but she'd been more concerned with making her safe place, her nest. Now she knew there wasn't any such thing. She didn't have a single safety net, not her business, not her own place.

It should make her more afraid. It didn't.

She pointed to a box of clothes. "Take that one?"

"You got it." Gabe hoisted the box to his shoulder. "Let's get out of here before the night is completely blown."

"Where are we going?"

He wanted to surprise her, wanted to show her where they'd been. "Things change and grow, Sailor. People and places, they aren't static. You see me as the person I was eight years ago, and I want you to see me now, today."

"Okay, Gabe." She bit her bottom lip, probably

trying not to tell him how wrong he was about what she thought about him.

Gabe wheeled the Hummer onto the street and gunned the big motor. "Just give me a minute and you'll understand."

A few miles later, they turned into their old neighborhood, onto the street where Gabe grew up. He still got a pang of something like regret, but since it was a daily occurrence now, it didn't bother him nearly as much as the first time he'd driven this block after his mother and father had been killed by a vagrant looking for money four years ago. "I closed down the shelter. My mom and dad tried their best. I think I've come around to that now. They did what they could for other people. What they could just didn't include me."

"Did you sell it to the developer?"

He glanced sideways. What would she think of him when she knew? "No."

"Then what—*you* built these condos?"

"My dad may not have been able to figure out how to make ends meet in the ministry, but he owned nearly the whole city block here, and what there was, I inherited. I tore down all the rattletrap buildings. With the money my grandparents left me plus what I made in Africa, I hired a contractor who specializes in building condos in lower-income areas."

"They're beautiful, Gabe. They look like little beach cottages with the bright colors and white trim. The streetlamps. Can you imagine if we'd grown up in one of these instead of those old row houses? I'd have felt like a princess."

Saving some other little girl from the kind of childhood Sailor had suffered. Yeah, it had crossed his mind. Maybe that made him a sap, but he was a sap with a ridiculously large tax shelter.

He turned the corner that would take him around the block to the street where she'd lived growing up. Her chatter came to an abrupt halt.

"I don't want to go there, Gabe."

He pulled to the curb, reaching for her hand, tugging on it until she looked at him instead of at her lap. "Do you trust me?"

She didn't speak for a long minute and he was about to put the car in gear and take her back to Cruse's house when she said in a very sure voice, "I trust you."

He pulled around the block to the construction site. Her house old house had been leveled. Two months ago, he had broken ground for a new set of lower-income condos. They were going up fast, but tonight the job site was empty and dark.

She sniffed. "You bought this block, too."

He hadn't bought this one for his parents.

When he pulled up to the gate, the security guard stepped forward with a hand up. He recognized Gabe and waved them through with a smile.

"I can't believe you did this. It already looks like a neighborhood." She touched his arm and he slowed the car so he could turn and look at her. "It's amazing, Gabe. What you've done. I'm stunned."

With a ghost of a smile, Gabe opened his door and ran around the car to open hers. He'd been planning to bring her here since practically the first moment he saw her, but now that they were here, he had nuts and bolts churning in his stomach.

The fence backing the housing development had once been a rusty chain-link fence that she and Gabe had escaped through into the wooded area between the two neighborhoods. Gabe had recently replaced the rusty chain-link fence with a high iron decorative fence.

He eventually intended to turn the wooded area into a park for the two housing developments. Not yet, though. He'd needed to keep it for himself for a while. The trails led to the creek bottom and the big old oak tree that had been his and Sailor's special place. He unlocked a gate that had been camouflaged in the iron fence and pulled her through it into the darker, cooler woods.

She sent him a suspicious look as the trail opened in front of her, but she stepped onto it. It beckoned her, like it always did him. There was something magical about this place, about the memories it held.

Going deeper into the woods, she caught her breath. "Oh, Gabe."

He'd been working on it in his free time for months, building up loosely organized beds along the trails and adding plantings native to Florida—flowering lantana and green, lush ferns. Tiny beveled lamps lighted the path, shimmering like tiny fireflies in the trees.

Sailor laced her fingers through his, wandering farther down the trail and across the little wooden bridge he'd built over the spring-fed creek. He'd had that cleaned, too. Instead of the trashy, somewhat polluted creek they'd grown up with, it was clear and pure, bubbling and gurgling.

He had an office in his condo. But more often than not he found himself here, under the trees where he and

Sailor had played and grown up and fallen in love. He hadn't understood it, but he hadn't been wrong. There was something, something about her, something between them he hadn't been able to shake.

He'd given her all he had as a teenager. He might've been young, but still a man, and once he'd given his heart, he couldn't just steal it back. It belonged to her then.

And now, after being with her again, seeing what an amazing, strong woman she'd become, he knew his heart would always be hers.

The big oak stretched its arms overhead. He sank to the ground on a carpet of fallen leaves, bringing her with him to lean against the trunk under the shelter of the ancient tree. "It's good, isn't it?"

She shook her head, still disbelieving. "It's absolutely incredible. I can't believe the transformation." She turned to look into his eyes. "You're doing an amazing thing, Gabriel Sloan."

He shifted. "Don't give me praise I don't deserve. All these changes are mostly motivated out of selfishness. I've made a lot of money. I needed a tax shelter."

"I don't think so." Her teeth caught on her bottom lip as she studied him. "You did this for your mom and dad."

She got so close and had always been able to see through him. "In a way. There was a part of me that wanted something tangible here to show I understood what they were about. Even if they weren't here to see it."

"Your parents were proud of you, Gabe. They always loved you."

"It's just a business, Sailor."

"If that's the case, then why build it anonymously? So you had money. Most people would have torn the shelter down and built apartments or something. What you've done is thoughtful and generous and simply miraculous." She nestled her head in the crook of his shoulder.

"I was trying to prove something."

"What's that?" Her voice had a dreamy quality. The moonlight dappling through the leaves of the oak made it seem as if they were in another world, just like when they were kids and escaping the world they lived in for another world altogether.

"That things change—they don't have to stay the same." He gestured to the woods around them and the condos behind him. "One day this will be a nice place for a kid to grow up. All things can become new— sometimes it's an outer change like this, but it doesn't always have to be. Sometimes it's an inner change. We've changed, thanks to someone giving us an opportunity, to a God who didn't give up on us. We're not the same people we were. *We* deserve a second chance, just like this place. Isn't it time we gave us that chance?"

She hugged her knees to her, looking down the stream toward the place where she had lived. "After all that happened then, and after I came back here looking for you, I felt wrecked, like my mother's boyfriend had broken me when he raped me. Like I had changed and couldn't be put back together." She drew in a deep breath as if she needed courage for her next statement. "Pieces of me were changed forever that night, Gabe."

He slid his hand down the silk of her hair. "I know, sweetheart."

Gabe reached into his pocket and pulled out the tin ring Sailor had been wearing around her neck all these years, the ring he'd been given with her belongings at the hospital. He held it out to her.

"I thought I'd lost it." She closed her fist around it, bringing it to her chest.

He slid his hand back in his pocket and brought out the one he'd been carrying for the last eight years. "I kept mine, too."

"Love, loyalty and friendship. Isn't that what the claddagh stands for?" Her eyes searched his in the light from the full moon.

Gabe pulled Sailor to her feet, her bright red skirt swirling around her legs. "We had all of those at one time, Sailor, or I thought we did. There've been some years to come between us. But there's no place for guilt—or shame—for what happened. We both have regrets. Now it's time to move on, to start fresh."

He bent and dipped the rings in the cold spring water of the creek, rinsing the dust and lint from the metal surface, bringing them up a little shinier to glint in the ambient light of the full moon. "I'd like for you to wear this again, if you want to."

She closed her eyes, and a tear crept out to slide down the curve of her cheek. "Are you sure?"

"I've never been more sure of anything."

Her green eyes, when she opened them again, were brilliant. She held out her left hand and he slid the ring on.

He handed her his ring, his heart squeezing in his chest as she took his large left hand in both of her smaller ones and slid the ring onto his ring finger.

There were no words spoken, no promises. They'd made those before, but the feeling, in his heart at least, was that he'd come home—finally, he'd found the place he'd searched for. He folded her into his arms, holding her there, where *she* belonged.

ELEVEN

The next afternoon, Sailor stood on the balcony of the tiny apartment topping Gabe's bayfront office, looking out over the water. Gabe had insisted she move locations yet again. Not being predictable—an easy way to stay a step ahead of the people who were after her. A shiver skittered up her spine.

The north wind had picked up, dropping the temperature since last night, so she'd grabbed a thick sweater and some jeans from the stash she'd brought from Sip This. She couldn't feel the chill. But she shivered anyway.

Gabe made it seem so easy. *Take this ring, pick up our lives*. Could it really be that simple?

Last night with him had been magical. No playful romp through the trees, this was it for her. *He* was it for her.

She wanted this relationship to work. She did. In the harsh winter daylight, she just wasn't sure it would. Things didn't come that easy to her, relationships didn't last in her life. As far as marriage went, who did she even have to model it on? Her mom? Yeah, that was a brilliant idea…if she wanted a long string of rotten, abusive men like the one who had raped her.

Charlie and Layla had come closer, but even they hadn't been able to tie the knot. Cruse and Bayley had made it work, but they were the exception rather than the rule.

Knowing things were stacked against them didn't make her a fatalist. It made her a realist. She pressed her lips together. The glass doors slid open behind her. Ever resourceful, Gabe came out with three hurricane globes he'd dug up from somewhere. "Now we can light the candles you brought."

With the little shells set into the base of the candles, they were bestsellers in the tiny gift shop at Sip This. "The tourists love these. I'm always having to back order them with Island Accessories."

"That's Layla's business, isn't that what you said?"

"She actually started her company with these, hand-pouring them and setting the shells. They were so popular with tourists, she added other things to her list—picture frames and other decorative pieces. All very tasteful, of course."

"Of course."

"Now she has a factory of sorts to assemble everything and she ships all over the country."

"Why are we talking about Layla?" Gabe slid his hand under her hair, resting it on the base of her neck. "When there are so many other things we could be talking about?"

Sailor knew she was babbling and avoiding the real subject on her mind. But she was caught up in fear, fear of being left behind. She'd never known her father. Her mother had been present—in body—but had never chosen Sailor, not ever, over feeding her addiction. Charlie…maybe Charlie hadn't left her on purpose, but he'd chosen his path, as well. She stared blankly at the bay. The water, so often a balm, did nothing to ease her anxiety. Instead, the boats bobbing in the marina below seemed to echo her restlessness.

Gabe pulled her close, blocking the wind with his body. "Honey, I know this waiting is tough. It seems like nothing is happening, but Cruse is working on this, and Maria, too, behind the scenes. Something will break. It just takes time, discovering the right piece of information. That is the key to it all. We'll get there, I promise. My first priority right now is keeping you safe."

"I know. It is hard, but I've had some time to think, too, and that's not all bad. It's not the waiting that's bothering me."

Fear flashed in his eyes, but he shuttered it so quickly she almost missed it, would have if she hadn't been watching him so closely. How sick was it that it made her feel the tiniest bit better that he was just as afraid as she?

"I'm scared." Drawing in a deep breath, she resolved to herself to be honest, not to run away from what he made her feel. "I don't know how to trust…*this. Us.* In my mind, I know nothing that happened to us was actually our fault, but in my gut, I have a hard time believing it."

When her voice shook, he turned her toward him and wrapped her sweater double around her, and then followed it with his arms, pulling her to him.

"I don't know if I would change the past if I could.

We lost eight years. But if we took back those years, there'd be no career in the Army, no Kitengi, no *Emily*.

"Sailor, I'd give just about anything to have the time back that we lost, but what if the road we've been on, what if it was the path we needed to take to bring us to this point? So we could be together the way we were meant to be?"

Sailor stared into his eyes, measuring him, as if maybe she could read his mind if she looked long enough.

"I'm afraid, too, Sailor." His voice rumbled through the emotional admission. "Afraid you'll change your mind, that you'll walk away again, that working this out will be too hard. But I've given this relationship to God, and I have to trust that He knows what's right for us even when we're not sure we can see the way."

"You're right. I've been looking to the past for guidance for the future when I really should be looking to God for answers. I'm sorry, Gabe." She said what she knew to be true, but somewhere inside were still doubts. So many times she'd wanted to believe, and so many times she'd been let down.

"Honey, I can't say anything that will make you believe in me. I can't put enough words together to convince you that what we have is forever. But I love you. There's nothing you can do that will change that. And I will be here, every day, proving it to you. I promise I will."

The candles on the table behind them sputtered and crackled. With his arm still around Sailor, he walked to the candle and blew it out. Picking up the lighter wand, he tried lighting it again. Again it sputtered and sparked and this time smoked out.

Sailor bent over to study the candle. "We need to check that out. If the manufacturer is skimping on the wick, I need to let Layla know. I can't sell those in my shop, not like that."

Gabe leaned down to pull his backup knife from its sheath. He picked up one of the candles and cut into it to see where the wick ended. "Maybe it's a defect or maybe someone made the wick too short to cut some corners."

Sailor thought Gabe would have to push hard to cut through the wax, but the knife sliced right into it. Understanding dawning on his face, Gabe cut more carefully around the circumference of the candle.

Breaking it open like an egg, he slid the contents—a bag of white powder—onto the outdoor table.

"Whoa. Is that what I think it is?" Sailor took a step back, away from the bag.

"Yeah. Cocaine or heroin. I don't know the exact substance, but I think we just found the answer to why Charlie was killed."

Sailor looked around. Unless she missed her guess, they had a fortune of illegal drugs on the table. "Maybe we should talk about this inside."

She picked up the remaining candles, taking them cautiously into the apartment and leaving him to deal with the bag of powder. He picked it up, squeezing it in his hand.

She closed the glass door behind him as he entered the room. "So now we know why Charlie was murdered. But who killed him?"

"I have a sneaking suspicion a certain southern diva is in it a little deeper than we would like to think. Walk me through what you know about Layla."

"Layla?"

"She's been at the fringes of this from the beginning. She and Charlie and Kenny, a little family circle of dysfunction." As he spoke, Gabe booted up his laptop. "I've got the original background checks on everyone involved in yours and Charlie's life. Layla's didn't pop anything. I'd have remembered that."

"What does it say?" Sailor ditched the candles and inched closer to Gabe, angling for a closer view of the computer screen.

"There are no red flags, but that in itself should've been a flag. Everyone has something—a call to the police for a neighbor's drunk and disorderly, an overlooked traffic ticket, a juvenile arrest at a party, *something*. But nothing in Layla's file called attention to her. She stayed under the radar."

"I just can't believe it's *Layla*. She's, like, in the Junior League, you know?"

"Yeah, I do." Gabe clicked on the e-mail icon. His in-box flooded.

"Man, I really have been preoccupied." He crinkled a smile at Sailor. "I wouldn't change my priorities, though."

"What's that?" She pointed to an attachment.

"Joe greased a few palms in Jamaica and apparently found someone able to scrounge up the police report from the murder in Montego Bay so many years ago."

It didn't look like much to Sailor, but she wasn't exactly experienced at reading police reports. Skimming over Gabe's shoulder, she saw that Joe had somehow obtained digital photos of the evidence file.

Aside from the physical evidence in the case, there were two photos—one of Charlie with a much younger Jamaican boss, and one of the girl Charlie had loved.

Gabe pointed at the girl. "Take a look at this and tell me who it looks like."

"She looks familiar. You don't think—"

"Think twenty years older with hair streaked gold." He raised an eyebrow at her.

"Mercy. If you gave her a modern haircut, that *is* Layla."

"My guess is he was so in love with her back then he told her where he was going when he left Jamaica. She's probably been blackmailing him into doing what she wanted all these years. There's no way of knowing for sure, but once you've gotten someone to kill for you, it's a small matter to blackmail them into doing lots of other nasty things."

"She's evil."

"It's beginning to look that way to me, though I doubt Charlie saw it from that perspective. Do you mind if we cut this short? I have a friend on the DEA task force who will want to see this."

Before Gabe finished his sentence, the security alarm in the apartment beeped quietly. They were too late. Layla's hit men had found them.

Already in motion, Gabe picked up his weapons, checking their ammunition. His sidearm and backup— and from a case Sailor hadn't even known he had, an assault rifle. Gabe slung the rifle over his shoulder.

Sailor stood next to the window, her fingers clenched on the frame. "I can see three down below. They're circling the building."

"Stay away from the window. We need to get out of here. Check the front closet and grab us both a warm jacket or coat or something."

Not frozen in fear, though her heart was pounding at an unbelievable rate, she did exactly what he said, putting on her coat so she'd have her hands free.

"This time we're going by water." He held a remote for a boat lift in one hand. "I've got my *Sea Ray* docked at the marina. It's already halfway down, but I can't let it all the way down until I can see it. I'm going to be honest with you, Sailor. It's a long shot, but it's the best option we've got."

Another dump of adrenaline sent her pulse skyrocketing. "It's okay, Gabe. I'll be fine."

"First we have to get out of the building. Do exactly what I say, don't question me, just do it. Okay?"

She nodded.

He pressed his backup piece into her hand. "Use it if you need it."

He'd already checked the load, but she checked it again. He gave her a taut nod of approval. "Ready?"

"Yes."

Gabe had a handheld unit with the security feed, but the picture was grainy and gray. The targets they wanted to avoid looked like black blobs. The stairwell to the second-floor office was clear. He put a finger to his lips and carefully opened the door.

They made it down one floor before, on-screen, Gabe saw the assassins coming up. He pulled Sailor through the door into the second-story office suite. He pushed her behind him into the corner and readied himself for the two attackers to come through the door.

Sailor held her breath. The gun she held was heavy in her two-fisted grip.

Booted footsteps hesitated, then moved on. Gabe laced an arm around Sailor's neck, breathing into her ear. "We can't wait. When they realize we're not there, they'll search the building."

Every silent breath was a reminder of the precariousness of their situation, but she still managed to keep her voice steady. "I'm ready, let's go."

Two agonizing minutes later, they arrived at the hardened outside door. "The boat is the last one on the left. When you get there, dive in and stay on the floor. We're gonna take off fast. You don't want to be standing up." He hesitated. "There will be someone posted outside. Our best bet is surprise."

Gabe looked into her eyes. He dragged her to him, pressed a hard kiss to her lips. "Run fast, Sailor."

She went first, but she could hear him running down the path behind her. In the fading afternoon light, the trees lining the property were shadows, blending and melding, the perfect spot for someone to hide. Fifty feet from the boat. Almost there.

Behind her, Gabe triggered the remote for the lift to lower it farther into the water. It creaked and groaned with the weight of the large boat.

A shout echoed from the balcony of the apartment. A bullet splintered the wooden decking at her feet. Out of time.

"Run for the boat, Sailor, the one on the end." Gabe sprayed cover behind them as he backed down the pier toward the boat. When she yelled, he released the trigger and turned and ran himself.

As he leaped into the stern, he grabbed life jackets off a nail on a post by the boat and tossed one to Sailor. "Get down."

He slammed the throttle into reverse and the huge engines roared. As soon as they were clear of the posts of the shed, he forced the stick forward. "Come on, baby, come on."

The engines caught and they shot forward. Flashes came from the balcony and the corner of his building. Shooting still. Pock marks splashed in the water, but not close enough. And in about ten seconds, if they were lucky, she and Gabe would be out of range altogether.

Sailor looked up from the floorboard. Pure speed and adrenaline. The look was carved on Gabe's face. Wind whipped his hair away from his forehead. He stood steady despite the bouncing speed, one foot in the seat, so he could see over the spray hitting the windshield. They were away. Under fire, but away.

She eased into a sitting position. "Are we clear?"

"Yeah, I think so," he yelled over the noise of the engine. "I can use a spotter. You up for it?"

The bay had a chop from the north wind, the jostling motion beating her up, so the seat would be a reprieve. She slid into it, buckling the red life jacket she hadn't had time to hook earlier. "Nothing—we're still clear—wait."

"Talk to me, Sailor."

Out of one of the canals lining the waterfront came a dark speedboat, navy blue or black, low to the water, superfast, shooting up a rooster tail. There was another one right behind it. "We've got two boats on our six."

Gabe whipped his head around, hair flying forward,

his muttered words lost in the wind before he slid down in the seat in front of the wheel. "C'mon, baby, c'mon."

As the boats drew closer, Sailor could see the men inside them. The one nearest her was huge, and armed to the nines. "They have guns, Gabe, some kind of sub-machine gun."

Gabe spared a fraction of a second for a how-in-the-the-world-do-you-know-that look. She shrugged. She had a cop brother who was always leaving stupid *Modern Warrior* magazines around, and she felt guilty if she threw them away before she looked at them. Besides, she kind of liked guns, liked the way she felt safe knowing how to handle them. She'd spent a lot of time at the range with her brother's friends.

Regardless of the weapon, it was time for her to get down. She tried to stay low—not that a fiberglass hull would provide much protection.

Gunfire spattered along the water beside them— what if the gas tank blew? "Yikes."

Gabe swung the nose into a high-speed curve, trying to throw off their aim. He succeeded, at least for the moment, the bullets from the first pursuer going off into a harmless arc. The second craft moved to cut them off, but Gabe leaned forward, pushing the stick as far as it would go. It didn't seem possible, but he coaxed a few more miles per hour out of the already taxed engines. The *Sea Ray* bounced across the tops of the waves.

With every jounce, Sailor bounced up. In danger of flying out of the boat and into the inky depths of the bay, she wrapped a tie-off rope around her wrist, anchoring it in her palm.

Gabe slid the rifle from his shoulder and began

shooting at their pursuers in short bursts while trying to drive. Stubborn man. Sailor jolted forward. "Gabe, give me the gun or let me drive. You can't do both!"

His eyes met hers, brown turning almost black in the intensity of the moment, before he slapped his weapon into her hand, eyes widening briefly as she turned and fired another burst from the seat parallel to Gabe. He laughed out loud. "I so totally love you."

She gulped. He'd said it before, when he'd been trying to calm her down. But the way he tossed it off just now without really thinking about it—that's the way people did who really had feelings, feelings they were comfortable with.

That scared her, made her all the more afraid of letting him down again. Heaven help her, she was more of a mess right at this moment than she'd been eight years ago. How could she trust her judgment? And even more scary, what if they died and she never had the chance to figure it all out?

Bullets chewed up the water from both directions. Sailor laid down return fire. They'd taken a few hits, but none in strategic areas. Thank God the shots hadn't hit the engines, but they were inboard and slightly protected.

Gabe steered toward the shore, screaming across the water. Through eyes slitted against the wind, Sailor could see the openings of several canals, and the huge houses that lined the waterfront. Lights were blinking on as the daylight waned. Soon they'd be driving blind.

And if anything, the area they were in was even more dangerous than the open water—filled with hurricane debris, old piers and even boats, the remains of a neighborhood that had never been rebuilt.

"There's debris in the water here, Gabe!"

"I know."

He stayed his course, but slowed just enough to allow their pursuers to move in. Sailor could see the cold, flat eyes of the man on the near side.

"They're getting closer. Gabe!" She kept a constant barrage of bullets flying, but there were two of them and only one of her. With one hand, Gabe fired at the second boat, keeping his other hand on the wheel and his eyes securely fastened on a point ahead in the water.

A bullet shattered the windshield and Sailor ducked. "Gabe, be careful!"

She glanced back again as Gabe yelled, "Hold on and get ready to fire."

He slammed the wheel to the hard left and then back to the right, straightening them out. The craft following them hit the hull of a submerged sailboat just barely visible under the water and shot up into the air.

Sailor fired a steady stream as the boat went airborne, arcing toward the water. As it hit, it made a creaking sound and exploded in a violent splash of orange-and-yellow heat.

Gabe forced the throttle fully forward. Their vessel responded, leaping ahead again. Sailor lifted her head up, bringing the rifle up with her to shoot at the remaining pursuer.

The guy behind them was lifting a rocket launcher. She let out a low, vehement word and Gabe whipped his head around.

He pulled the steering wheel hard to the left, and grabbed her hand. "Time to bail out."

* * *

The water's freezing, was Gabe's first thought. His second was panic that he'd lost hold of Sailor's hand.

He surfaced, looking for her, his life jacket's buoyancy keeping him easily afloat. The smoldering wreckage, some pieces still burning, rained from the sky. He didn't see her. They'd been going so fast. What if she'd been knocked out by the force of the water? Disoriented himself, he looked frantically around. He couldn't call for her. Bad guys still had to be in the neighborhood.

Catching a glimpse of red floating about forty feet away, his heart plummeted. Her life jacket. *Dear God, please let her be alive.*

His clothes dragged at him as he swam, but he pushed the water and debris out of the way with long, hard strokes. In seconds he knew.

She wasn't attached to the life jacket.

Where was she?

He picked up the jacket. Did her zipper break? The buckles?

No.

Horror spread like a black fungus through him. The buckles' straps had been sliced clean through. Cut.

The low thrum of a motor cruising up behind him drew his attention. Slowly, he turned his head around. The boat that had been chasing them down the bay idled a few feet away, carrying two black-clad men armed to the teeth. In the stern, Sailor stood dripping, her blond hair whipping in the wind like a flag. A third assailant had a matte black gun shoved into the soft skin under her chin.

Oh, Sailor.

They'd gotten to her first, fishing her out of the water before he could even find her. He couldn't see her expression, couldn't see if she was afraid or angry. If he had to guess, knowing Sailor, he'd figure royally peeved.

With his eyes fixed on Sailor's, he almost missed the movement from the other side of her, but he caught sight of the gun rising to a shooting position. He dove under the water, nearly numb fingers fumbling with the buckles and zipper on his life jacket. It released, rocketing upward, allowing him to swim farther under. Not fast enough, though. A sharp sting cut across his foot, still too close to the surface of the water.

His lungs burned, but he needed to get as close to shore as possible before he came up for air. If he could get to a pier and hide in the shade of the pilings, so much the better.

He kicked out, a new worry niggling at his mind. The dusk hours were feeding time for sharks and even in the bay's brackish waters, sharks were plentiful.

Hypothermia, sharks. This night had become an unholy mess. He couldn't even let his mind skip to Sailor and what she might be going through. He had to think and plan one logical step at a time.

Gabe surfaced. Dark shapes like creepy bridges stretched over the water, less choppy here in the protected area close to shore. He looked back. The people chasing him had gone. With Sailor.

He swam to the end of the nearest pier, praying for a ladder. Thankfully, there was one, and he scrambled up on bare feet.

No lights shone from the house or pier. If luck was with him, the owners weren't residents, but weekenders.

Their shed would provide shelter from the wind until he could get help. From the back pocket of his tactical vest, he pulled a waterproof bag containing the drug packages, a small black GPS device and his cell phone.

With one punch of a button, the phone dialed Cruse.

"Conyers."

Guilt lodged in Gabe's stomach, a solid knot of regret and wishes. "Cruse."

"Gabe, what's happened?"

Of course, Cruse would know instantly. He closed his eyes. "They took Sailor. I need help, Cruse. To get her back."

"What do you need?"

"A ride. Clothes. Weapons. Not necessarily in that order." Quickly he filled Cruse in on the drug find in the candles, and their assumption Layla was involved.

"Hold on a second." Murmured conversation. "I'll be there in ten minutes. I've got people from the DEA task force in my office with some interesting information from 'friends' in Colombia that could have bearing on this situation."

"What information?"

"There's a big shipment coming in, one of the largest ever for this area. Apparently the buyer here decided to expand the business. Maybe why things suddenly got dicey here?"

"Makes sense. They're trying to protect their pipeline. And they're very anxious to find out how much Sailor and I have found out on our fishing expeditions. What time?"

"We don't have an exact time. The informant wasn't giving that up."

"I'm going in for her."

"*What?* Don't be stupid, Gabe. Risking two lives isn't better than risking one." Over the phone, he heard Cruse swallow hard. "Even if that one is my sister. We're going in within hours. We'll get her out."

"Cruse, if I wait, the chances are good she'll get caught in the cross fire. She's an innocent and she has no idea what's coming. I'm not leaving her to face that alone."

"We only have a general idea of where the shipment is coming in along the waterfront. There's no way you'll find her before the task force."

"You're wrong about that." Gabe picked up the black GPS device. The glowing green dot had gone from blinking to steady. "I know exactly where she is."

TWELVE

Sailor squirmed closer to the desk on the hard floor. Her captors had brought her to a warehouse, or maybe an abandoned marina, somewhere on the waterfront, tying the boat off at a huge concrete pier. She'd discovered while still on board that struggling wouldn't get her anything except hurt. Her eye still stung where the big, hairy guy had punched her.

The tiny room they'd thrown her in eeked dark, damp cold. No furniture except an old desk and chair with no seat, both rusting out from the salty sea air. The only window was very high, maybe fifteen feet, and crusty. The weak light filtering in from the outside was barely enough to let her see the room, but at least enough to keep her from going mad.

She lifted her head to squint at the window again. Maybe she could reach it if she piled the chair on the desk. She went back to working on her hands, scraping the rope across the rusty surface of the desk, thanking God she'd had the good sense to get a tetanus shot after the last hurricane.

She'd replayed over and over again her last glimpse

of Gabe. He'd been right there, looking into her eyes, sending her a message. When the bad guy started shooting, he'd dived down under the water, and that was the last she'd seen of him.

The shooter didn't think Gabe could have escaped injury, not with the unbelievable amount of fire he'd discharged into the water. He even said he'd seen blood in the water. Sailor prayed Gabe made it. Not for her rescue, although she acknowledged that would be nice, but because she needed to say something to him.

She hadn't told him she loved him.

He'd told her. Several times, in several different ways. And in many more ways than in words—and she'd repaid him with misgivings, with distrust, with angst and fear.

No more.

She was done with the past. It hadn't been pretty. But it had shaped them into the people they were. The man she loved was very different from the boy she'd been infatuated with in high school. She was no longer a girl who hid from things. She had made hard choices to protect those she loved. It was time she made the hardest choice of all.

She'd learned to trust God for her safety. He offered more—more adventure, more love, more life. But she had to make the choice to follow Him. To risk it all for a life that wasn't safe, but spectacular.

To risk everything for the man she loved. Gabe needed to know she loved him—passionately, furiously, and without reservation.

Moses and Jehoshaphat, would this rope never break? They always made it look so easy on TV. Jack

Bauer, or MacGyver, they'd have been through this rope in two seconds.

Footsteps. Clonking across the concrete outside in the hall except for intermittent clanking on the metal drains. Sailor'd managed to keep the apprehension at bay by hanging on to her mad, but a shiver of fear crawled up her spine.

Common sense told her they wouldn't have kept her alive if they didn't think they could use her. But an hour ago they were trying to kill her, so how useful could she really be? She shivered again. Freezing, not scared, because if she was scared, she might not be able to act when she needed to.

The door slammed open.

Layla stood there in her little suit, high heels and all, with her henchmen.

Sailor kept her head down, but one thought upended another in her mind. Accusing Layla of anything outright wouldn't help. Acting stupid seemed to be the most prudent course of action.

"Layla, oh my, I'm so glad you're here." She gushed, letting one word tumble over the other. "There were guns, and explosions, and oh, Layla, these men kidnapped me and brought me here. I'm so glad to see you."

Her voice trailed off as the woman stepped forward. Layla had been a friend, or close. Her eyes, a mild blue, cornflower almost, were usually so guileless. Tonight they were blank of feeling, cold and sharp. Her light floral perfume overlaid the smell of diesel fuel and brackish water.

Sailor pinched her fingers together. "What's wrong? Aren't you here to help me?"

"Can the act, Sailor." The savvy businesswoman jerked her head toward the men behind her and they grabbed Sailor's arms, one on each side, wrenching her to her feet. Muscles cramped too long in a folded position protested as her weight landed full on them.

Layla circled her. "It's actually lucky for me that you survived the explosion. Instead of moving my whole operation after tonight, I can find out what you know. And what you know is what the cops know. Like your brother and that boyfriend of yours. Right?"

Sailor blinked, a slow, innocent drop. "I don't know what you're talking about, Layla. Please, stop this."

Real consternation filled her voice. Layla crazy was scary enough. But the fact that she was brilliant enough to have hidden it all these years—that terrified Sailor.

The goons dragged her into the empty warehouse—empty except for a bank of computers in one corner, with someone she couldn't see bent over one of them. The cavernous room had been dim when the kidnappers brought their boat in. It was brightly lit now, with halogen lights gleaming off the deep water canal that split the storage area down the middle.

They pulled her all the way to the edge of that black water and turned her back to it. Layla got close. "Tell me what the cops knows about my business."

"Layla, I—"

"*Don't* tell me you don't know what I'm talking about. Ken the idiot thought he could make some extra money selling candles out of Sip This to some of his former customers, but I know you opened the box. Some candles were missing. *What* did you tell the cops about the business?"

"Nothing. I swear...I don't know what you're talk-ing about."

Layla nodded at the hired muscle standing beside her. Before she could guard herself, he punched her in the stomach. She doubled over, unbelievable pain in her midsection, bright colors swirling behind her eyes. She gagged, trying to control the pain, but the man kicked her in the side.

She hit the water. Gasping one quick breath in, she went under. *Oh, dear God, help.* Her hands were still tied. She worked them furiously, kicking with her feet to the surface of the oily water. The rope wouldn't budge.

Coughing, she came up. A gaff hook maneuvered toward her and dragged her out of the water, gouging her skin in the process. Fear snaked its way in. She fought it back as she lay shaking and shivering at the edge of the canal.

Layla's pewter-gray sharp-toed shoes came into her line of sight. "I'll ask you again. What do the cops know?"

She couldn't tell. Any time she could buy them was more time they'd have to catch this woman. She had to keep the fear at bay, had to stay strong. The longer she made Layla beg for information, the longer the police and the DEA would have to build a case.

"Sailor, just in case you haven't noticed, I'm not playing."

One of the goons snickered. Layla kicked out with those viciously pointed shoes, catching Sailor just under the eye.

"Tell me!"

Her cheekbone split. Blood ran down. The only thing Sailor could think to do was tell Layla a part of what she knew. Something that might appease her but wouldn't damage the operation, whatever it was.

And the sad truth? Sailor didn't know enough to save her life if Layla really wanted to kill her. She'd been in protective custody with Gabe. All she knew was what Gabe had told her at Sip This early this morning.

"They know there's a connection between Ken's office and the drugs. They know the ballistics match from a guy who was killed in Ken's office and the one that killed Charlie." Maybe that would make Layla think the hammer was coming down on Ken Banks, not her.

"Ms. Grady, I've got an e-mail here from the gentlemen delivering our shipment? They'll be in earlier than expected."

"Did you confirm the source?"

"Yes, ma'am."

The voice sounded familiar. Sailor lifted her head and tried to focus eyes that seemed just as determined to blur. But she saw what she thought she'd heard. The person she'd tried to save from a life of hardship had done her wrong.

"Chloe?" Sharp disappointment in the betrayal speared through Sailor. What could you expect from people? The path of least resistance always seemed like the right way to go. It had always worked that way for her mom.

Chloe shrugged, a semi-apologetic look on her face before she ducked behind the computer screens again.

Layla laughed. "Turns out your little street waif has a knack with computers. She's very impressive. And remarkably easy to control. Amazing how helpful a little addiction can be."

The guards pulled Sailor to a standing position, blood and water joining to puddle at her feet.

"I'm a very busy woman, Sailor. I need to know one thing before you rest for a while. Where are the drugs you stole from me?"

"I didn't—"

"Yes, you did. My men found the empty candles in the apartment where you were. Now tell me where the packages are."

Sailor's head drooped. She was so tired. The thoughts she'd had of stalling, of somehow outsmarting Layla—she couldn't even figure out what she'd wanted to do. "Last time I saw them, they were on the kitchen table. I don't know what happened after that."

She felt rather than saw Layla nod at the goon to her left. His fist connected with her jaw, whipping her head around. Her eyes squeezed shut with the effort of holding her brain in her head. Oh, mercy, she hurt.

Her body started to fall and she couldn't do anything to stop it. And then, nothing but blackness.

Gabe walked silently onto a tiny dirt road, his meeting place with Cruse. There were thousands of roads cut into the woods around northwest Florida. It was still recent history that Emerald County had been mostly wetlands. Developers had brought in mountains of fill dirt and built neighborhoods out of swamps to fill the desire of the masses to live on the Florida coastline.

Fortunately, no hint of the usually busy summer traffic remained tonight. The bayside road was dead quiet. He could almost believe he was alone out here. But he knew better.

Glancing around, he pressed back the panic for Sailor, to get to her, to hold her. The fear that she was being hurt, or worse. He was doing everything he could for her. If he went in unprepared or without a plan they would both be in worse danger.

But, oh God, what if?

He hadn't been there for her once when she'd been so terribly hurt. He'd lost her then. What if this time there were no second chances?

Focus, Gabe. He needed every bit of his expertise. He'd done this before, in Ecuador. Before he worked in Africa, he and his team of for-hire commandos had rescued a thirteen-year-old American girl who'd been snatched from a compound close to the Colombian border.

He could get Sailor out. But he had to focus on the job, not the person, not what he stood to lose. *Sailor.*

Cruse melted out of the forest into his line of sight. "Gabe."

"Cruse. What's the latest word?"

Cruse shook his head. "No change. They're still planning on going in when the supplier reaches the warehouse."

He stopped, looked back at Gabe, letting his worry and fear for his sister show in his eyes, green like Sailor's. "I'm going to need the coordinates of the warehouse."

Gabe pulled the GPS out of the waterproof bag. His

hands were frozen and stiff, not working right after his swim in the cold bay. He flipped through the screens and then passed the GPS monitor to Cruse. "I hid the tracker in her clothes."

Pulling a large pack off his back, Cruse dropped it onto the ground. "You need to get some dry clothes on before you're hypothermic."

A hard chill shuddered through Gabe. "May be too late for that."

"There's a Thermos of coffee in there. Not as good as Sailor's, but I don't think you're in a position to complain."

Gabe forced a smile. Donning a dry sweatshirt and jeans, he opened the Thermos, swigging the strong, hot brew. He wiped his mouth with the back of his hand. "Thanks. Better already."

Cruse tossed surfer hair back from his face. "What made you think to put a tracker on Sailor?"

Gabe took another long swallow of coffee. "I was captured by rebel fighters in Africa. Had I not been wearing a GPS tracker, I would have been dead before my team could find me. As it was…"

The memories always overwhelmed his composure. No matter where or when, they swamped his senses like a storm surge. "As it was, I had to be carried out and spent four months in the hospital."

Cruse didn't hand out sympathy, a trait Gabe could respect. Instead his steady, serious gaze met Gabe's. "Are you sure you want to go in alone?"

"What's the alternative? Letting Sailor stay in there on her own? I don't think so."

"I've got some equipment for you." A bulletproof

vest was first out of the bag. "It's the thinnest we had, but it'll provide some protection."

Gabe nodded, taking it, feeling the heft of it. He'd have preferred not wearing it at all, but he'd be taking a bigger gamble with Sailor's life if they shot him and he didn't survive. "I need a weapon. I lost everything."

Cruse started unbuckling his belt.

"I don't think that's going to work, Cruse."

His lieutenant shot him a look, and his low chuckle rolled out. "It's the belt buckle. I had a friend who's a leather worker make it a few years back for when I need a concealed weapon that's really concealed. There's a curved blade buried in the leather. The trigger is here." Cruse pointed.

Gabe peered into the bag. "I'd feel a lot more comfortable going in with one of those."

"You can hide those outside before you go in. The FBI apparently has somebody on the inside who they're in contact with. They've gotten a message through to be on the lookout for you. Layla's crew is gonna be nervous, wanting to get rid of Sailor."

"Do I have a way in?"

"The agent will find you lurking outside the building. Instant credibility for the agent. Instant incarceration for you."

"Hopefully with Sailor."

"If you can stall them long enough to let the task force get into place, everybody will be happy, a lot of drugs will be off the streets, and a major pipeline will be shut down before it gets off the ground. Win-win-win."

"And Sailor will be safe."

"Win." Cruse's voice had gone husky with suppressed emotion. "Gabe, I can see how you feel about her. She's lucky to have someone to care this much."

Gabe swallowed hard before he could push words out around the lump in his throat. "Can't you convince the task force to take this group down another night, when there's not a citizen involved?"

"No way. Normally, Layla's crew takes out one of Charlie's charter boats on a late-night tuna run. Except instead of coolers full of fish, they come back with coolers full of coke. Her business is the distribution through her tourist stuff. Some of the souvenir items are totally legit, and she doesn't run any money through her own interests. She leaves that to the people she blackmails into helping her."

"Like Charlie."

"Exactly. That's why she's been so hard to catch."

"And Ken?"

Cruse reached for the empty Thermos. "As far as we can tell, he's just a dealer in way over his head."

"Still, that doesn't tell me what the big deal is about tonight."

"Tonight Layla's meeting with her boss. Instead of middle men meeting to transfer the cocaine with the charter boats, the coke's coming in on a big yacht. U.S. Coast Guard tracked it from Venezuela starting a week ago. If the DEA strikes tonight, they get Layla and the pipeline to the U.S., but they also get her up-line, the link from South America. It's a chance they're not likely to get again."

Cruse zipped up the bag. "Last piece of equipment is a wireless earpiece. It's not completely reliable, but you'll hopefully be able to hear the chatter and know what's going on. One last thing, Gabe. If I say 'abort,' please listen. The DEA won't hesitate to take you out if you're jeopardizing their mission."

"Got it." Gabe held his hand out to shake the hand of his lieutenant, friend, and if Gabe had anything to do with it, soon-to-be brother.

Swinging up his pack, Cruse started back for the woods and his transport but hesitated, placing a finger to his ear and turning back to Gabe. His face was carved with graven lines in the dark shadow of the trees. "I'm sorry, Gabe. The plan has changed. The task force is going to take control of the boat before it reaches the rendezvous point. There's too much chance the supplier will escape if he makes land."

"You should go. You're part of that task force."

"Right." Cruse placed a hand on Gabe's shoulder. "Go with God, brother. I'm praying for you."

"You, too."

Cruse nodded and, turning, strode down the dirt road disappearing into the knotty pine forest. In a few seconds, Gabe heard the powerful engine of Cruse's Jeep rumble away.

He lifted his eyes to the dark night sky. Three or four stars blinked in the blackness. His hope felt like those few stars, a weak light in the distance.

He couldn't think about Sailor and what she might be going through. All he could do was what he had trained for, year after year. He whispered a prayer, a heartfelt supplication that God would give him the strength for the task ahead. He was good at his job.

And it was time to go to work.

* * *

Gabe eyed the rattletrap waterfront warehouse from his prone position in the pine needles in the edge of the wooded lot. It didn't look like much. In fact, if he hadn't had the GPS reading, he'd have driven right past the place and never taken a second look. With the night-vision gear Cruse had brought him, though, he could see light beaming out of every tiny crack and crevice. That building was definitely occupied.

A door on the side of the building slammed open, blinding him with the sudden bright flash in the N-V goggles. He threw his arm up to cover his eyes. A few seconds for his eyes to adjust and he looked again. The green view through the lenses was crystal clear. No color, but the woman who'd stepped out of the building proved to be easily identifiable, her white beanie unmistakable. Chloe, the little chick Sailor had "saved" by giving her a job in the coffee shop. Apparently, her FBI job had her connected to the drug task force, as well.

She leaned against the side of the warehouse, cupped her hand around a lighter and cigarette. Puffed. The picture of a nonchalant criminal out for a late-evening smoke. But when she kicked off the wall and strolled closer, he saw a different look etched on her face. Shrewd, cunning.

Still with the cigarette, she walked toward him. Right toward him. Several times she stopped, turned slightly back toward the warehouse and listened. Each time, unerringly, she continued toward his hiding spot, until her feet stopped not twelve inches from his face.

Chloe shouldered up to a tree, staring into the distance toward the water. She tossed the cigarette down about an inch from his fingers and leaned toward his face as she ground it out with her foot. "You follow my lead or you're on your own."

"Agreed." Until she put her agenda in front of Sailor's safety, or until he decided he didn't want to.

"Sailor's in the northwest corner of the building. She's hurt, but it's not as bad as it could be. Not yet."

Gabe's stomach pitched. And his determination to take Layla down grew. He flipped off the N-V gear and packed them back in his bag. "Wh—"

When the door opened again unexpectedly, Chloe kicked him in the face, surprising him. Her hauling him up by the collar of his borrowed Gap sweatshirt and toward the door with a tiny, businesslike gun under his chin didn't surprise him at all.

A big, ugly bruiser of a man stood in the door. "Ms. Grady says you need to get back to work." He stared at Gabe. "Who's that?"

Chloe gave Bruiser snotty teenager attitude. "All you need to know is the boss will want to see what I found hiding in the bushes. Go get her."

"How many?" Gabe said it under his breath, so the words wouldn't carry.

"Three." She rubbed the back of her hand over her nose, and sniffed. She played her part well. He'd give her that. "And Layla."

From the darkness on the other side of the warehouse, heels came tapping. Layla Grady with her coiffed hair and her tidy little suit, her two rottweiler henchmen trotting along beside her. Junkyard dogs—they were scarred up, muscled up, and snarling.

He hadn't seen Sailor yet. If she'd seen him when he

came in, she would've called out. Could she be hurt worse than Chloe said? The thought of it made his blood run cold. He wanted more than anything to hunt for her, to grab her up and run like crazy from this madness.

But more than ever before, he had to focus. He couldn't take his mind off the job in front of him, because if he did, she would die.

"Gabe Sloan." Layla shook her head, circling around him, fondling a small silver gun in her hand. "How sweet of you to come. Chloe, tie him up and then I want you and Roper to go outside and make sure he was alone."

Scarface slammed Gabe against one of the supports of the warehouse. Chloe unbuckled Gabe's belt, sliding it from its loops.

Gabe clenched his jaw, muscles bunching. "This may sound like a cliché, Layla, but you do know you aren't going to get away with what you're doing, right?"

She laughed in his face. Her eyes were blank, soulless voids. She'd used people for years for her own gain. She wouldn't hesitate to kill him and Sailor if she had to. He could not underestimate her. "Of course I'm going to get away with it. And Gabe, you're going to help me by telling me what you know."

Chloe cinched the belt around his hands, leaving the buckle just in the reach of his fingers. He didn't know how she knew. Maybe it was the message from Cruse, or maybe it was just blind luck, but whatever it was, it might be just the thing that got him and Sailor out of this goatfest alive.

"You can beat me all you want, Layla. I'm not telling you one thing." Layla didn't have to know he'd sell his own soul if he had to in order to get Sailor out of here in one piece.

"Oh, Gabe. I'm not going to lay a hand on you." Layla's smile scared the living daylights out of him. "Boys?"

One of the muscle-bound creeps strode over to the corner, the one where Chloe had said Sailor was being held. His eyes saw a pile of rags on the floor, but when Scarface kicked it, it moved. *Oh, Sailor.*

The brute dragged her up by her shirt. She blinked against the hard overhead lights, and staggered to her feet, her hair matted and dirty, blood caked and dried on her face and clothes.

They'd hurt his woman, hurt her badly. Gabe felt black rage fill him, and every bit of resolve he had hardened into steel. He would not be outsmarted. He would not be beaten. Somebody was going to pay tonight. And it wasn't going to be him.

Sailor didn't open her eyes when the voices roused her from her thug-induced sleep. Didn't lift her head, either. She wasn't sure she could. The cold had seeped so far into her bones that she wasn't even shivering anymore, she just hurt.

But she could still pray. And she prayed like crazy for Gabe's safety and that she would have a chance to escape.

Testing, she wiggled first her feet and then her hands. Tied—from her position, she thought probably to a chair. But she wasn't back in the tiny office. She'd been left in the big room, because she could hear the murmur of voices and an undercurrent of tense excitement that hadn't been there before.

She cracked an eye, the one that wasn't swollen from the cut, but she couldn't see over the pile of stuff in front of her. Eyes closed, she worked her abused, cramped muscles, tensing one group at a time, trying to keep the blood flow up. And still she worked her wrists against the chafing ropes, but the skin had swollen. Tears came to her eyes at the futility of her efforts.

Pain exploded in her ribs, streaked through the rest of her body. She curled in as much as she could, tied to the chair, but she couldn't protect herself as she was hauled to her feet and cut loose from the seat. Relief felt more like agony as blood rushed to parts of her arms and hands that had been without. She gritted her teeth against the throbbing.

The goon dragged her, hobbling behind him, back to the middle of the room. The chill she felt from her bones became a soul-deep ache. Layla was going to kill her. The only reason she was alive now was Layla wanted to learn what she knew.

The taste of torture Sailor had gotten had been just that—a taste. There was more to come. Then they'd kill her. She'd never see Gabe again, never have the chance to show him how she felt about him, never be able to hold him, to actually say the words.

She wanted to scream. Panic bared its teeth inside her, rearing up like some wild thing. But she had to manage her fear. She had to gain control. If she didn't, she might as well be dead right now.

The evil jerk Layla had doing her dirty work grabbed Sailor's hair and forced her head up. She opened her eyes and looked right into Gabe's.

Her heart stuttered for a second, she would've sworn

it. Not for a million dollars would she have wanted him here, in her own private hell, but oh man, was she glad to see him. He had a bruise swelling on one cheekbone, but he looked so incredibly good. *Alive*.

Layla circled Sailor, the floral aroma of her perfume wafting in her wake. "I have a little problem, Sailor. You don't want to talk and Gabe says he won't talk."

She shook her head, waving the little silver gun. "But one of you is going to have to spill it."

Like lightning, she snapped the gun across Gabe's other cheek, laying it open. Sailor cried out, lunging toward him, but Layla whirled around, jamming the gun under Sailor's chin.

"Look, Gabe. Look at her." Layla's voice whipped out, cold and sharp. "She's bad off. She probably has internal injuries. She can't take any more."

Sailor stared into Gabe's eyes, willing him to see what she held inside. All the love, all the strength. Her fear was gone. She would do what she had to do. His nod was so slight she almost missed it.

The depths of those caramel eyes beckoned her, warm and liquid. She'd looked into them too many times to be mistaken. They'd always been able to tell what the other one was thinking. She saw his muscles bunch. And felt more than heard the words, *on three*. He blinked, one slow blink.

Two. Three.

She dropped her entire body weight, throwing Layla off balance and grabbed the shooting arm, as Layla got one wild shot off. Out of the corner of her one good eye, she saw Gabe sling his belt around, catching the guy with the scar around the neck.

Sailor's pain had faded, gone in the blitz of adrenaline that downloaded into her system. She flipped Layla over her head the way she'd been taught in her self-defense classes, never letting go of that gun hand. When the woman landed with an "ooph" on her back, Sailor rolled over her to gain more leverage.

Staring into Layla's hate-filled eyes, Sailor realized again that—for so long—she'd been living in a make-believe world. *Make believe everything is fine and it will be. Make believe you're safe and you are.* That kind of life wasn't for her, not anymore. She knew for a fact God had more for her than that.

She slammed Layla's shooting arm into the concrete warehouse floor once, twice, and again, until Layla released the weapon to skitter across the floor.

Sailor wasn't a victim and she wasn't going to live a victim's life, hiding away from sorrow. Yeah, living life was way more painful than surviving it, but it was incredibly more beautiful, too.

The wannabe drug lord screamed for her henchmen, bucking and flailing underneath Sailor. Sailor glanced up. One of Layla's sidekicks lay out cold beside the support pole where Gabe had been tied up. Gabe fought hand to hand with the other one on the other side of the pole.

Layla reared up, scrabbling for purchase with one stocking-clad foot and one foot still bearing her four-inch pump. Sailor slammed her fist in Layla's face. Layla's head snapped back to the concrete floor with a hollow thud. She made a halfhearted motion to rise again, but with that headache, she'd probably be down for quite a while.

Sailor rolled to her feet. Gabe…

She started for him. A small shuffle behind her alerted her. She swung around, her leg instinctively in motion, her roundhouse kick knocking Layla back to the floor where she lay still and prone. The police or FBI or whoever wanted her would have no trouble with her now.

When Sailor turned around, Gabe waited for her. Standing strong even after taking out two overmuscled thugs. She fell into his arms, holding on for all she was worth. She hadn't even known he was still alive, but here he was, solid and real beneath her hands. Nothing on earth had ever, ever felt quite this good.

He buried his face in her hair. He was shaking. "I'm sorry. I'm so sorry, Sailor."

She pulled back, sliding her hands up to hold his face in her hands. "What are you sorry for?"

"I let them take you. You were all alone. You must have felt like I abandoned you all over again."

"No, Gabe. *No.* I knew if there was any way possible you would come after me. You did. Here you are. You came to rescue me."

"No dice, honey. We rescued each other." He shook his head, not letting her give him the credit for this one. "You had my back and I had yours. And that's the way it's going to be from now on if I have any say about it."

He touched her battered face, his eyes shimmering with what she realized were tears, for her. "They hurt you."

"Yeah, they did. But I'm strong. I realized it through this whole ordeal. They can beat me up on the outside, but they can't get to me here." She touched her heart with the palm of her hand. "Not anymore. You're the only one who has that power. I love you, Gabriel Sloan."

A slow smile spread over Gabe's face. "I wasn't sure I'd ever hear you say that."

"Yeah? Well, you did. And here's another bulletin for you. I'm going to say it again. Every day, for as long as you'll let me."

Gabe lifted her off her feet, prepared to hold her forever. Never had he expected her to be so fully ready to embrace a life with him.

She yelped, a quick whimper she tried to hide, but he put her quickly down on her feet. "What's wrong?"

Her breaths were quick and shallow. "The ribs. It's no big deal."

"Oh, honey." With one finger, he eased the hair back from her bruised face. "All right, that's enough. We're getting out of here and getting you to the hospital."

"What about Chloe and Hairy Guy?"

The door slammed open. Chloe walked through it. When she pulled off the ever-present white beanie, the brown curly hair went with it, and a cascade of shiny red hair came tumbling down. "Hairy Guy's dead, the EMTs are en route, and Team Two just picked up Ken Banks."

Sailor's mouth dropped open. She looked at Gabe.

"FBI." He pulled Sailor close, back into his arms, gently, more careful of her ribs this time. He wasn't ever going to let her go again, not if she had anything to do with it.

Tenderly, he pressed a kiss to her sweet lips. Not a deep, soulful kiss—just a reminder that they had lots of years to enjoy kisses together.

"Can't you guys cut me a break here?"

When Sailor laughed and pressed her lips to Gabe's again, Chloe groaned.

"That does it. I'm waiting for backup outside." Chloe backed away from her job of securing Layla and her henchmen, the noise outside signaling that her FBI backup had arrived on-scene.

Sailor sighed, a soft, satisfied sound. "So, you think we can go home now?"

"I guess your house is out of the question."

She smiled at him, and the thought crossed her mind that anywhere he was felt a lot like home.

"I don't really care where we go. I'm finally going to be carrying my bride over the threshold. Whatever threshold is handy. Yours, mine, Cruse's. I'll carry you over the threshold of the local tattoo parlor if that's where you want to go." Gabe scooped her up. "How about we make my house ours?"

She flung her arms around his neck and rested her head against his shoulder. "The old neighborhood? Sounds absolutely perfect to me."

EPILOGUE

"You're all packed?"

Gabe lifted his head from the baseball glove he was oiling. "Just a few more things to finish up." Then he saw her face. "What's wrong?"

She held out a brightly colored trifolded card. Her eyes were bright, nearly feverish. "Take a look."

"Pajama Diva Sleepover?" Gabe tipped a smile. "Aren't you a little old?"

"It's for Emily. She's turning eight this month." Sailor blinked, the tears coming more quickly to her these days. Gabe had gotten used to the lightning-fast changes and kept tissues in his pocket.

The handwritten note from Emily's adoptive mother invited them to join the party for cake and ice cream. He studied her face. "We'll be back from Orlando. Do you want to go?"

"Do you think she'll want to meet me?"

"Oh, darlin', of course she will. She'll love you." He pulled her onto his lap, squeezing her gently. "We'll buy her a fabulous present at Disney World."

"Okay." Her hands shook as she took the invitation

from him, smoothing the folds. "I can't believe I'm going to be with her, to get to see her up close."

"Believe it, sweetheart. Soon enough, you'll be up to your eyeballs in squealing eight-year-old girls." He faked a shudder.

Sailor smiled and hugged him close. "Sounds like heaven."

She pulled back to look at her watch. "We probably need to get going. Gabe, are you sure you have the time to take this trip now?"

The trip was his Christmas present from Sailor—a whole week at spring training with many of the major league teams, training in Orlando or within driving distance. A chance to add to his signed baseball collection and a trip to Disney World. It was perfect, and he wouldn't miss it for the world. Especially with his amazing wife.

"I've got plenty of time. With the grand opening of the condos over, I can take some leave."

"But Joe—"

"Joe has other backup besides me, honey. And I wouldn't miss this trip for anything. Did you get your bikini?"

"I don't think I'll fit in that one." She laughed as she slid from his lap and crossed to the window to look at the ocean, the spring-green water, crystal-blue sky.

Gabe tossed the glove on the side table and went to stand behind her, sliding his hands around to the slight bump of her abdomen. "Hi, baby."

The wonder of it still overwhelmed him, that under his hands was a baby the two of them had made. A miracle, Sailor had said. Ask him, she was the miracle.

"You don't think I'm fat?"

Now that was a land-mine question if he'd ever heard one, but thankfully, he knew the right answer. "I love you any way you are, Sailor. A little rounder, a little fuller. You're gorgeous. Of course, I thought you were beautiful with pigtails and zits."

She flopped back on the bed and he followed, propping on an elbow and sliding one of his big, dark hands around her still-tiny ribs, enjoying the contrast. Only five months pregnant now, she'd get a lot bigger. He'd enjoy her then, too.

When she looked into his eyes, hers were suspiciously moist. He grabbed her hands and brought them to his chest.

"Hey, honey. We don't have to go if you don't want to. What's wrong?"

She blinked three times fast to clear her eyes, and sniffed. "These ridiculous hormones. Nothing's wrong. I love you, Gabe. I never would have had the courage to buy Ken Banks's share of the coffee shop and add the gallery if it weren't for you. I never would've known I wanted to."

She could feel the beating of his heart under her hands, strong and steady. "From the beginning, skinned knees and ripped jeans to drug dealers and coffee shops, you've been able to see through all the cover to what's inside. To see *me*. Nobody else ever has." The depth of him, this man who fought for right in the world, would never cease to amaze her. He was tough and smart, but most of all, he was decent. And that decency drove him to do what he did, to set right what little he could.

He made her world right.

His hands smelled like the leather of his baseball glove as they cupped her face. "I love you, babe."

"I know." She still felt the wonder of it sometimes. Still felt the incredible blessing they'd been given to have a second chance at love.

He smoothed a kiss to her temple and lifted the hair off her neck, letting his lips roam. He reached her mouth and his lips joined hers in a sweet, soft kiss.

"Gabe." She sighed.

He snuggled her against him. "You know you're incredible. Artist, wife, mother…amazing."

She laughed. "So amazing you didn't ever want to see me again."

"Are you going to bring this up every day?"

"Only for the next sixty years or so."

Gabe tucked her under his arm and pulled her close. "I can live with that."

* * * * *

Dear Reader,

In *Moving Target* Sailor Conyers bravely built a new life after being viciously attacked. Gabe Sloan found a way to forgive his neglectful parents and build a legacy of hope out of a decaying neighborhood.

Both Gabe and Sailor had found God faithful through some tough times, but were they living life to the fullest? It took being separated from Gabe and believing she may never see him again for Sailor to realize how much she loved him—how much she was willing to risk to love him.

Many of us are just survivors, making it through life one day at a time, sometimes one hour at a time. But God wants so much more for us. Jesus said, "I came that you might have life and have it abundantly." (John 10:10)

My prayer for you is that you discover the life God has for you—a life worth risking everything for.

I'd love to hear from you! Please contact me at newtonwriter@gmail.com or visit my Web site: www.stephanienewton.net.

All God's best,

Stephanie Newton

QUESTIONS FOR DISCUSSION

1. Sailor was helped and nurtured by someone after a tragic event in her life. Is there someone in your life that you look up to as a mentor and friend? Why are those people important in our Christian walk?

2. Gabe thought he had it all together, but a call to his former fiancée's house sends him reeling. Have you ever been blindsided like that? How could Gabe have avoided that reaction?

3. In some way, Sailor blames Gabe for his father's callous words. Do we take responsibility for our family's actions? Should we?

4. In Sailor's past is an alcoholic mother and an abusive "family" member. She has coping mechanisms in place that help her to deal with the hurts of the past. What are some of the ways she deals with her fear? What does she have to learn from God before she can let go of that fear?

5. Gabe owned the property where his parents ran a homeless shelter. How was he able to take something that had been painful in his past and turn it into something positive for his future?

6. Sailor had always loved painting and color—but she felt that gift had been taken away from her by

her abuser. Why does she finally pick up a paint-brush again? How does it make her feel?

7. What did Gabe do with the property where Sailor lived, and where he and Sailor had played together as children? Why was it so important to him that he show it to her?

8. Sailor made a very difficult decision to place a child with adoptive parents. Charlie helped her as a pregnant teen. How did Gabe choose to support her years later? How can we choose to support others in the same, or similar situations?

9. It took a whole team of people to keep Sailor safe. Gabe, Maria, Cruse, Bayley, even Chloe. Have you ever had to depend on others for something when you're used to depending on yourself? How did that make you feel?

10. Gabe and Sailor kept the promise rings they'd given each other in adolescence. They became one more symbol of how things old and tarnished can be given new life and a new chance to shine. But can clinging to things of the past sometimes hold us back from God's best?

11. In *Moving Target*, Gabe learns that love is worth waiting for. He reminds Sailor that if they had been together all those years they would have missed out on some of the most important moments of their lives. Maybe it was the journey that God meant for

them to take. What are you waiting for in God's timing?

12. Sailor learns that life is more dangerous lived to the fullest, but it is definitely more beautiful and satisfying, too. Maybe it's an art class, a visit to a homeless shelter, or a phone call to a person who might be a friend—is there something you are afraid of, that you just need to take a step of faith to accomplish?

*A thrilling romance between a British nurse and
an American cowboy on the African plains*

Turn the page for a sneak preview of
THE MAVERICK'S BRIDE
by Catherine Palmer
Available September 2009
from Love Inspired® Historical

Adam hoisted himself onto the balcony, swinging one leg at a time over the rail. He hoped he hadn't been spotted by a compound guard.

But the sight of Emma Pickering peering out from behind the curtain put his concerns to rest. He had done the right thing.

"Good morning, Miss Pickering." He leaned against the white window frame.

"Mr. King." She was almost breathless. "I cannot speak with you."

"But I need to talk. Mind if I come inside?"

"Indeed, sir, you may not take another step! Are you mad?"

He couldn't hold back a grin. "No more than most. I figure anyone who would leave home and travel all the way to Africa has to be a little off-kilter."

"You refer to me, I suppose? I'll have you know I'm here for a very good reason."

"Railway inspection, is it? Or nursing?"

Emma looked even better than he had thought she might—and he had thought about her a lot.

"Speaking of nursing," he ventured.

"Mr. King, I have already told you I'm unavailable. Now please let yourself down by that…that rope thing, and—"

"My lasso?"

"You must go down again, sir. This is unseemly."

Emma was edgy this morning. Almost frightened. Different from the bold young woman he had met yesterday.

He couldn't let that concern him. Last night after he left the consulate, he had made up his mind to keep things strictly business with Emma Pickering.

"I'll leave after I've had my say," he told her. "This is important."

"Speak quickly, sir. My father must not find you here."

"With all due respect, Emma, do you think I'm concerned about what your father thinks?"

"You may not care, but I do. What do you want from me?"

"I need a nurse."

"A nurse? Are you ill?"

"Not for me. I have a friend—at my ranch."

Her eyes deepened in concern as she let the curtain drop a little. "What sort of illness does your friend have? Can you describe it?"

Adam looked away. How could he explain the situation without scaring her off?

"It's not an illness. It's more like…"

Searching for the right words, he turned back to Emma. But at the first full sight of her face, he reached through the open window and pulled the curtain out of her hands.

"Emma, what happened to you?" He caught her arm and drew her toward him. "Who did this?"

She raised her hand in a vain effort to cover her cheek and eye. "It's nothing," she protested, trying to back away. "Please, Mr. King, you must not…"

Even as she tried to speak, he stepped through the balcony door and gathered her into his arms. Brushing back the hair from her cheek, he noted the swelling and the darkening stain around it.

"Emma," he growled. "Who did this to you?"

She fell motionless, silent in his embrace. No wonder she had shied like a scared colt. She hadn't wanted him to know.

Torn with dismay that anyone would ever harm this beautiful woman, he felt an irresistible urge to kiss her.

"Emma, you have to tell me…." Realization flooded through him. A pompous, nattily dressed English railroad tycoon had struck his own daughter.

"Leave me, I beg you. You have no place here."

"Emma, wait. Listen to me." Adam caught her wrists and pulled her back toward him. He'd never been a man to think things through too carefully. He did what felt right.

"I want you to come with me," he told her. "I need your help. Let's go right now. Emma, I'll take care of you."

"I don't need anyone to take care of me," she shot back. "God is watching over me."

"Emma!" Both turned toward the open door where Emma's sister stood, eyes wide.

"Emma, go with him!" Cissy crossed the room toward them. "Run away with him, Emma. It's your chance to escape—to become a nurse, as you've always wanted. You'll be safe at last, and you can have your dream."

Emma turned back to Adam.

"Come on," he urged her. "Let's get moving."

* * * * *

*Will Emma run away with Adam and finally
realize her dreams of becoming a nurse?
Find out in THE MAVERICK'S BRIDE,
available in September 2009
only from Love Inspired® Historical.*

Love Inspired. HISTORICAL

INSPIRATIONAL HISTORICAL ROMANCE

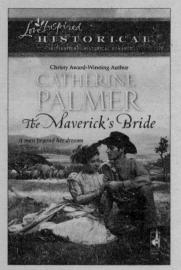

Emma Pickering is drawn to Adam King, the rugged cowboy she meets upon arriving in East Africa. The man is as compelling as he is mysterious. And if he'll agree to a marriage of convenience, it would solve both their problems. Yet their match is anything but "convenient" when Emma's fears gain hold, and malicious whispers threaten to tear the couple apart.

Look for
The Maverick's Bride

by Christy Award-Winning author

CATHERINE PALMER

*Available September 2009
wherever books are sold.*

www.SteepleHill.com

REQUEST YOUR FREE BOOKS!

2 FREE RIVETING INSPIRATIONAL NOVELS
PLUS 2 FREE MYSTERY GIFTS

YES! Please send me 2 FREE Love Inspired® Suspense novels and my 2 FREE mystery gifts (gifts are worth about $10). After receiving them, if I don't wish to receive any more books, I can return the shipping statement marked "cancel". If I don't cancel, I will receive 4 brand-new novels every month and be billed just $4.24 per book in the U.S. or $4.74 per book in Canada. That's a savings of over 20% off the cover price. It's quite a bargain! Shipping and handling is just 50¢ per book.* I understand that accepting the 2 free books and gifts places me under no obligation to buy anything. I can always return a shipment and cancel at any time. Even if I never buy another book, the two free books and gifts are mine to keep forever.

123 IDN EYM2   323 IDN EYNE

Name	(PLEASE PRINT)	
Address		Apt. #
City	State/Prov.	Zip/Postal Code

Signature (if under 18, a parent or guardian must sign)

Mail to Steeple Hill Reader Service:
IN U.S.A.: P.O. Box 1867, Buffalo, NY 14240-1867
IN CANADA: P.O. Box 609, Fort Erie, Ontario L2A 5X3

Not valid to current subscribers of Love Inspired Suspense books.

Want to try two free books from another series?
Call 1-800-873-8635 or visit www.morefreebooks.com

* Terms and prices subject to change without notice. Prices do not include applicable taxes. Sales tax applicable in N.Y. Canadian residents will be charged applicable provincial taxes and GST. Offer not valid in Quebec. This offer is limited to one order per household. All orders subject to approval. Credit or debit balances in a customer's account(s) may be offset by any other outstanding balance owed by or to the customer. Please allow 4 to 6 weeks for delivery. Offer available while quantities last.

Your Privacy: Steeple Hill Books is committed to protecting your privacy. Our Privacy Policy is available online at www.SteepleHill.com or upon request from the Reader Service. From time to time we make our lists of customers available to reputable third parties who may have a product or service of interest to you. If you would prefer we not share your name and address, please check here. ☐

LISUS09

Love Inspired SUSPENSE

TITLES AVAILABLE NEXT MONTH

Available September 8, 2009

FINAL EXPOSURE by Roxanne Rustand
Big Sky Secrets
Safety and serenity are what Jack Matthews seeks in
Lost Falls, Montana. But when Jack discovers that his
beautiful host, Erin Cole, is being stalked, how much will
Jack have to risk to keep her safe?

A SILENT FURY by Lynette Eason
One girl from the Palmetto Deaf School is dead, and another
has been taken. Detective Catelyn Clark will do anything to
save the kidnapped girl...even work with her ex, FBI agent
Joseph Santino.

RACE TO RESCUE by Dana Mentink
Her beloved brother is missing somewhere in the harsh
Arizona desert, but the police won't take Anita Teel's
fears seriously. Only one man will: Booker Scott, the
hardened rancher who broke her heart, and will have to risk
everything to help her now.

PROTECTOR'S HONOR by Kit Wilkinson
Why is someone trying to kill Tabitha Beaumont? That's
what NCIS agent Rory Farrell vows to find out. She needs
protection—Rory's protection—while Rory needs answers
Tabitha doesn't even realize she holds. Yet how can he find
the truth without betraying Tabitha's trust?